LUNA STATION
QUARTERLY

Issue 045 | March 2021

Editor-in-Chief
Jennifer Lyn Parsons

Editors

Rocky Breen • Anna Catalano • Linda Codega
Wanda Evans • Angelica Fyfe • Cathrin Hagey
Sarah Pauling • Cait Ryan • Carly Racklin • Shana Ross
Gô Shoemake • Margaret Stewart • Izzy Varju

LUNA STATION PRESS
NEW JERSEY

Luna Station Quarterly publishes short fiction on March 1st, June 1st,
September 1st, and December 1st. For more information and submission
guidelines, please visit our website at lunastationquarterly.com

For Luna Station Press

Creative Director - Tara Quinn Lindsey
Editor-in-Chief & Founder - Jennifer Lyn Parsons

LUNA STATION PRESS

www.lunastationpress.com

CONTENTS

Editorial

Jennifer Lyn Parsons

Jennifer Lyn Parsons is a writer, programmer, and maker. With influences ranging from Laura Ingalls Wilder to Jim Jarmusch, her tales feature a rare physicality with details that feel hand-carved. When not writing code or prose, she is also the editor-in-chief of the venerable Luna Station Quarterly. She finds joy in video games, comics books, discovering music new and old, and making things out of wool, paper, and wood.

Welcome to Luna Station Quarterly, year twelve.

I'm happy to tell you all that over the last decade plus, we've retained a child-like wonder and deep love of stories. Fairy tales still enchant us, science fiction still ignites our imaginations. Witches, rogues, explorers, and zombies lead us through the books we read and show us new and interesting ways to be human. Even in this strange new world we find ourselves living in, this life that we could not have imagined would look so drastically different a year ago, stories are still here for us.

I do what I can to keep these editorials as timeless as I am able, but I would be remiss if I didn't note that we have been under the cloud of the pandemic for a year now. I had just finished off the production work on last year's March issue when I fell ill myself. Recovery was longer than I expected, but I am grateful that, with time, I did indeed heal. I am so happy that you are here with us, too, reading these words now.

For me, it feels too soon to look back on the last year. We're still in it, after all. Hope is on the horizon and the promise of spring here in the North East feels even more potent than usual, especially as we've had more snow than in the last few years combined. Even as many of us joke that time does not exist anymore and we're somehow living the very long March 2020, I have LSQ to keep me on track. The steady cycle of LSQ's quarterly appearance marks time for me. This March is not last March.

How will the last year impact the stories we tell? As a publisher and author myself, that is one of the most interesting questions I consider now. Tales written in the last few months have begun to appear in our slush pile and I am rather pleased to say that there is wonder and adventure still to be had within our pages. The darkness has not swallowed the light and our collective creativity is still burning brightly.

So please take some time for yourself today to get a little lost in our pages. Allow these stories to show you possibilities and hope and strange new worlds or even a bit of old-fashioned fun. Let them be a buoy, for that is what stories excel at doing for us all. And this batch? Well, they're particularly good, if I do say so myself.

L S Q | 045

Mars Ascending

Hannah Whiteoak

Hannah Whiteoak is a writer of speculative short fiction and flash. Her work has appeared in Flash Fiction Online, Escape Pod, On The Premises, and various anthologies. Find her online at www.hannahwhiteoak.me or @hannahwhiteoak

Jupiter had fallen on the carpet. The basketball must have been too heavy for the twine. I picked up the planet, which had come to rest against a hardback copy of *Galactic Dynamics*. Its paint was chipped, a fleck missing from the centre of the Giant Red Spot. Perhaps I could fix it up.

The planetary mobile had been my gift to Jessie on her sixteenth birthday. Hoping to inspire her to apply for the Mars Academy program, I'd made the planets out of whatever I could find: fuzzy tennis balls, a volleyball I patched and pumped up, paper mache for the inner rockies. When it was ready, I'd led her to her bedroom, hands over her eyes.

She'd gasped as she'd taken in the eight planets, each hanging in a net of twine, around the paper light shade that stood in for the sun. To the ceiling I'd glued fragments of glass, which sparkled like stars. Mars took pride of place above her pillow, the white-painted colony bright against its red surface.

"Wow," she'd whispered. "Thanks, Dad."

Soon, images of nebulae had replaced the "save the whale" posters on Jessie's walls. I'd added more hooks to the ceiling so I could drape a net over her bed to keep out mosquitoes and framed a picture of her mother so she could keep it on her desk. No matter how high her homework towered, it never pushed Kathy out of place.

What would I get Jessie for her next birthday? When I was a kid, my parents would buy my older sisters makeup or new clothes, but you couldn't get hold of those now. By the time she turned eighteen next summer, my daughter might not even be on Earth.

I collected plates from the floor. We used to have a rule against Jessie eating in her room, but I'd let it slide. I'd let a lot of things slide lately. At least she didn't need nagging to make her study. Her sights were set on Mars.

I took Jupiter to my workshop, dropping off the plates on the way. I was glad I'd moved the kitchen to what had once been the spare bedroom as the room downstairs had flooded again a few weeks ago, and this time the water showed no signs of receding. Plumbing in the new sink hadn't been easy, but I'd hacked it together, and the house was so damp anyway we hardly noticed the leaks. Meanwhile, my workshop had moved from the garage to a floating shack I'd constructed from an old shipping container. Again, I berated myself for not having moved to higher ground while the house was still worth something. It was too late now.

There wasn't much space in the workshop. I'd been repairing the outboard motor on our neighbour's boat before I broke off this morning to take Jessie to school, and parts remained littered over the bench. I brushed them aside, feeling guilty. Laura would need that boat to get to her job at the hospital tomorrow. I didn't want her to put herself at risk wading through the deep waters downtown.

Since the floods started, most of our neighbourhood had emptied, families abandoning their rotting homes to take their chances in the camps, but Laura clung on next door.

"I could never leave my neighbours," she'd said, smiling shyly at me.

The damage to Jupiter wasn't extensive, but mixing the paints to match the exact shade of red proved tricky. I was at it for nearly an hour, using a pin to scratch dried-up flakes from each tube, mixing them with water to bring them back to life.

While the paint dried, I tinkered with the motor. Getting it running again was a straightforward task, but the fuel tank was beginning to corrode. I'd look out for a new one next time I went to the dock. For now, I used the last of a can of WD 40 to lubricate the moving parts.

By the time I'd finished, the Red Spot was dry to the touch. I carried the planet back to Jessie's room and hung it from its hook in a new twine hammock. Jupiter was restored.

***

Jessie had always been lean, but stress had made her skinny. Her mousy hair hung lank around her face—a consequence of the shampoo shortage, or a warning sign of malnutrition? I heaped rice onto her plate.

"Dad, I'm sick of rice."

"I know, but I couldn't get anything else. You need calories."

Jessie looked back down at the Mars Academy brochure. Glossy pictures showed students smiling inside their helmets as they clambered over rocks, each dressed in the school's uniform spacesuit.

"How's the studying going?" I asked.

She sighed. "It's really tough, Dad. There's so much to learn."

While politicians threw around blame, the world's richest conglomeration had started shipping the brightest young people to Mars to work on the colonisation project. Representatives had come to Jessie's school in her first year to encourage the best students to apply. Since then, she'd been obsessed with getting in.

"Just do your best. That's all anyone can ask."

"What if my best isn't good enough? What if I have to stay here?"

Earth was failing fast. We'd stopped referring to "freak" floods and started to accept the unpredictable surges and retreats of water. News reports had become dominated by images of refugees streaming across continents, reminding us we were the lucky ones. Last year, the TV signal had shut off altogether.

My daughter had no future here.

"Of course you're going to pass," I said. "You're top of your year. What did you get in your last test?"

She picked at the skin around her nails. "One hundred per cent."

"You're going to knock 'em dead."

"I hope so."

I knew I should be proud. She was going to make it. But I'd miss her. Already it felt like there was a second hole in my chest, its raw edges catching every time I breathed.

***

The next few weeks I barely saw Jessie. She holed up in her room studying. I brought food, leaving it outside her door so as not to break her concentration. When she was at school, I collected the empty plates.

Above her bed, Mars twisted slowly in the breeze from the open window. I wiped my brow. It was almost too hot to bear inside the house, and the solar panels on the roof didn't provide enough electricity to run the air conditioner. The power grid had shut off weeks ago, and no one could get hold of the company to find out if they would bother to restore it. None of the local radio stations reported the outage.

In the boat on the way to school, Jessie stared at the flooded streets, resisting my attempts at conversation. Stupid, really — all those years I spent fixing up other people's houses, many of them now ruined, when I could have been with her, figuring out how to relate. Money, I used to tell myself, that's what she needs. Now that the rich had their own currencies, locked away in blockchains, government-issued money wasn't worth the polymer it was printed on. You might as well burn it for fuel.

"Exams going well?" I asked, steering the boat around a floating car.

"I don't know," she said.

"You must have some idea."

"Dad, leave it."

With strong winds from the south rippling the water, the flooded streets reminded me of the beach holiday we took when Jessie was a toddler, back when air travel was a standard middle-class luxury. She'd run in and out of the waves in a yellow swimsuit, a floppy pink hat on her bonny curls.

Unusually, it wasn't raining today. Instead, a low-hanging sun burned orange through the haze. The hum of the underpowered motor provided a rich baseline under the cries of the gulls.

"I know you can do it," I said.

Her shoulders hunched as she coughed. She'd been coughing a lot lately, but whenever I asked she insisted she was fine.

How much did she remember of the early days, when the warnings didn't seem real? When wildfires raged across the news, Kathy and I took Jessie on climate marches and told her not to worry: the people had spoken, so things would soon change. Around the time she started secondary school, the floods became regular. We pretended it would all turn out alright. At first we bought sandbags, later boats.

"Dad?"

"Yes, love?"

"What will you do if I get into Mars Academy?"

"I'll be right here. You can call me whenever you want."

"Will you be OK?"

"Of course."

The motor sputtered. I whacked it with my palm, and it settled back into its steady hum.

"I won't get in anyway," she said. "The tests are too hard."

"You will. And I'm proud of you no matter what."

She frowned.

"Your mum would have been, too."

"Would she?" Jessie's hair streamed in the wind as she turned away. "She wanted me to look after you."

For weeks I'd been too angry to do anything other than drink. Our second child was born blue, cord wrapped around his neck, which was bad enough. I'd never thought it possible we'd lose Kathy too.

"Let me look after you," I said. "That's my job."

***

Over the next few weeks, a blanket of cloud settled over the city, reducing the power provided by the solar panels. The trickle of electricity they gave was just enough to run Jessie's computer. I'd managed to connect it to the internet by rigging up an extension to the phone lines across the street, whose poles hadn't yet succumbed to rot.

If I lived alone, I'd happily have let it go. The web was a painful reminder of how much better some people had it than us. *Comparison is the thief of joy*, I reminded myself often. But Jessie needed access for school, so I kept going out in the rain to fix the connection every time it failed.

Tensely, we waited for Jessie's results to post online. She paced around the house, scraping the last traces of peanut butter out of a jar. I retreated to the workshop, distracting myself with my latest project: a wind turbine to replace the failing solar panels. Along with torrential rainstorms, strong winds were a weather trend that seemed to be here to stay. The plan was to power not only our home but Laura's too.

Hearing a scream, I dropped my hammer and ran. "Jessie?"

When I threw open the door, tears were streaming down her face. My stomach lurched.

"I passed! Dad, I'm going to Mars!"

My heart leapt, but the joy was quickly drowned in a sick feeling. I steadied myself against the door frame. She was leaving.

I forced a smile onto my face.

"That's...that's brilliant." I tried to keep my voice from cracking. "Best news I've ever heard."

***

Jessie looked stunning in her silver spacesuit. Thanks to the superior nutrition provided by the Mars Academy training camp, the hollows in her cheeks had filled out. Every time I'd been able to get through on video calls, her smile had been wider, the creases between her eyebrows gradually smoothing out. Now, on launch day, she laughed. I realised I couldn't remember the last time I saw her laugh. Why had I not made sure we had more fun times together? Why had I made everything about getting her away?

"Five minutes until boarding."

It had been a difficult six months. The house was too quiet, as though it had gone into hibernation since Jessie left. Finally, it had woken with an almighty crash: the floor of my bedroom had rotted and collapsed. It wasn't clear how much longer the rest of the house would last, so Laura had insisted I move in with her.

"Four minutes until boarding."

I hadn't told Jessie. No need to bring up that old argument again. Of course I wasn't trying to replace her mother. But I needed to move on too. Couldn't she see that? My nails cut into my palms.

"Three minutes until boarding."

The trip to the launch site had been sickeningly comfortable. The Mars Academy team had picked me up in a shiny boat, which zipped through the water like an arrow into the future. My neighbours had glared as its movement caused waves to slap against the fragile walls of their homes.

"Two minutes until boarding."

Parents pressed their palms to the glass, reminding their kids to call home at the first opportunity. I hung back, clenching and unclenching my fists, while Jessie joked with her new friends.

"One minute until boarding. All students to gate now."

Jessie picked up her helmet and turned to me.

"Thanks, Dad."

That's all I get? I shoved the thought down. "You earned it, kid."

As I waved, she turned and walked through the gate that would take her onto the capsule. One of the gun-wielding guards smiled at the crowd of excited teenagers. I shouted, "Good luck!" but Jessie was talking with the other young astronauts and I don't think she heard. They disappeared without a backward glance.

***

On return from the launch, the Mars Academy boat stopped outside the old house I'd lived in with Jessie. The house sagged as if it knew I'd given up on it. Floorboards groaned as I climbed from the boat through an upstairs window. There was mould on the walls of what had temporarily been our kitchen. Something had recently scuttled along the counter, leaving tracks in the dust.

I tested each step as I walked along the landing, eyeing the splintery hole where my bedroom used to be. I thought of all the times I'd tiptoed this route with a plate of food that I'd leave outside Jessie's door, not wanting to disturb her study.

The door had warped in its frame. I had to shove my shoulder against it to make it open. When I burst into her room, my knuckles white around the hammer, the planets shivered as if in fear.

I swung with all the force I could muster. The paper sun imploded. Planets crashed, Saturn's rings crumpling as they hit the ground. Mercury rolled into a corner. Earth fell with a dead thump.

Only Mars was left. I swung again, and it toppled to the floor. Facing up was the miniature Academy I had painstakingly reproduced, dabbing white paint onto the red landscape to represent each massive dome. I brought the hammer down on top, hitting the planet over and over until it burst like an empty seed pod.

Exhausted, I dropped the hammer, sank to the floor, and sobbed among the destroyed worlds.

***

Laura was calling my name, but I didn't rise. I was tired of people needing me to fix things. Tired of them expecting me to be OK.

The house creaked and groaned. A planet rolled against my foot. A hand touched my shoulder.

"That must have been hard for you."

"It's best for her," I said.

"Let's hope so."

She put her arms around me. Her skin smelled sour with sweat. Funny, to think we once worried so much about the way we smelled and looked, buying all those plastic-packaged chemicals to hide behind. For us, there were no hiding places left.

"We shouldn't be here," Laura said. "The floor could collapse at any minute."

Posters crinkled at the edges. Old clothes Jessie had been too embarrassed to take to training camp slumped in dejected piles on the floor. The mosquito net hung limply over the ocean-themed bedding we'd picked out when she was twelve.

"We should take the sheets," I said. "I've been thinking of fitting a sail to the boat."

"Do you want to bring anything else?" She looked at the planets scattered over the floor. "Where's Mars?"

"Out of reach." I picked up a blue paper-mache ball daubed with green continents. It was squashed out of shape. "I guess we're stuck with this."

The Dragon Hunter's Daughter

Gabrielle Roselynn Dina

Gabrielle Dina is a fiction writer living in Pennsylvania. She earned a B.A. in Drama at Hofstra University, and is currently working on a full-length play. Her short fiction has previously appeared in Mirror Dance Magazine.

The Dragon's Riddle:
This creature's found with every flesh,
A joy in birth, a balm of death.
Wrought where even waters die,
Friend by tongue, and kin to I.

***

Many years from now, a man charges across an open green, seated high upon his steed with a lance tucked under his arm. The woman he rushes does not move at his approach, nor does she cry out in pain when his weapon finds its mark. He rides past, then brings his horse around with the expectation of seeing her dead. He will be sorely disappointed.

She stands tall, and with a languid motion, the lance is plucked from her breast and cast aside. She advances upon him; the eyes of his horse roll within their sockets in dumb animal fear, and that is the only warning he receives before his steed rears back, and he falls. When he manages to gain his bearings once more, his horse has long abandoned him, and the woman stands before him unharmed, not even a spot of blood upon her tunic. Her hand curls around the circumference of his neck, and she wrenches him off of his feet. He kicks out against empty air. One hand goes to her iron grip, the other toward his sword, but she unsheathes it for him and holds the point just over his left breast.

"If I attempt to pierce your heart, rest assured, I will be wildly more successful," she says. Her nails slice through the film of his flesh, drawing out pinpricks of blood.

"What kind of creature are you?" he gasps. For he has heard that she is, at best, a witch and a trickster, and at worst, an unholy beast—but not in all his wanderings did he hear tell she might be deathless. But she deigns not to answer him; instead, her grip loosens, and he is thrown to the ground.

"You will not be the last to try this," she informs him, "though, fortunately for me, you were not the first, either." Her fingers find the tear in her tunic that his lance made, and she rends it further to reveal what lies beneath. A fantastical sight greets his eyes. For the first time in his life, he is struck dumb with wonder.

"Shall I tell you a secret, Sir Knight?" she asks, "one my father taught to me?" She crouches before him, face to his face. One hand grips his chin, claws pinching the flesh of his cheeks, and he is forced to look into her green, green eyes.

"Once your heart has been broken that first time—and provided you survive it—another can never kill you," she whispers, her breath sweet again his skin, her smile sharp. "So, you should have gone for the head."

She lets him go. "Leave now," she tells him, "and you will live to fight another day. Go procure yourself another horse and a better lance. Come back and test your luck once more, if you so desire. But if you do, heed my advice. Aim straight and true. I will not be so merciful again." And then, with a rush of unnatural wind, she is gone.

He will scamper away to lick his wounds. He will seek out a new mount and a better weapon, and as he procures his supplies, his mind will return to her again and again until the hidden depths of her eyes are a well-worn memory. When they meet once more, on a different green, perhaps he will have taken her warning to heart. Perhaps this time, when he approaches her, he has a different goal entirely. But this is not that story. Not yet.

***

Once upon a time, there stood a solitary cottage in the meeting place betwixt a vast rolling steppe and the beginning of a deep, dark wood. The cottage was built into the side of a hill, and the man that lived inside it was an eccentric sort of fellow, silver-haired and bespectacled. He lived with his put-upon wife, and for many years it was just the two of them on the cusp of the wilds until at last they had three daughters—each more beautiful than the last, each one odder than the first. The first daughter was named Corvina, and she came into the world squalling her outrage at the unexpected, unwelcome change in habitat. Once she was situated in her mother's arms, her father came into the room to see his first-born daughter, her little cheeks still red from screams that would continue to echo about if not for her mother's breast. Her father looked upon her, and the joy of being gifted a child was so great that he could not help the tears streaming down his face, but all the same, he shook his head slightly and said to himself very quietly, so that his wife would not hear, "No, not the one."

The second daughter was named Dorata, and she too came out squalling, though not quite as loudly as her elder sister. Her father was overjoyed at the safe delivery of another precious daughter, but when he saw her in her mother's arms, he whispered to himself, "Almost."

The third daughter was named Meralda, and when she was born, not a sound issued from her lips. The most she would do was stare up at her mother with big green eyes and nary a peep, so resolute in her vow of silence that the midwife had to spank her to make sure she drew breath. When her father beheld her for the first time, he cried, as he had done twice before—but this time, in a loud, clear voice, he said, "Yes, her."

As the years turned, the three little girls grew into bigger girls, and each, in their own way, captured a special place in the heart of the town. Corvina was renowned for her midnight locks, her charming smile, and her clever long fingers. On market days in the town center, she could often be found amid a gaggle of young boys who hung on her every word as she entertained them with whimsical stories. Dorata, in contrast, grew to be fair-haired and light of foot. At the peak of midday in the hot, golden summers, she could be spotted running throughout the fields, her loose tresses trailing behind her. A pack of other children followed close behind her, girls and boys alike, each eager for a moment of her warm attention to alight on them alone. The third, Meralda, had her green, green eyes—and little else, for she was quiet and shy, hardly ever speaking. Not even childhood scrapes and bruises could induce her to wail. As a result, while her sisters attracted admiration and interest, Meralda inhabited the edges of their shadows. When she did venture with them into town, one would hardly know it. If one was particularly observant, one might catch an elusive glimpse of large emerald eyes peering around the corner of a building; or, within the town library of ancient leather-bound books, one might notice the soft displacement of air from small, careful breaths, the rustling of pages coming from a hidden nook, or the trail of deft fingers in dust—the only signs of her presence. The most observant of the townsfolk would note these signs and then nod to themselves and agree: ah yes, she is her father's daughter. The first two they had never been quite sure about, but in regards to Meralda, there was no doubt.

For, you must understand, Meralda's father had been just as quietly strange as Meralda in his youth, and age only cultivated his eccentricities. He charted the stars at night and walked through the woods from dusk until dawn. He spoke gibberish in rhymed couplets when the mood came upon him. He guarded the entrance to his personal library with an alarming zealousness and claimed to have all sorts of arcane, fantastical, impossible treasures hidden inside it.

He called himself the Dragon Hunter.

***

The first lesson her father ever taught her was to never tell her true name to a dragon. The second lesson was to never trust a dragon, for although it is against their principles to lie, that makes them twice as dangerous.

Her lessons started early, as soon as Meralda could stand and toddle about on wobbly little legs. She would follow the Dragon Hunter out into the forest, where he would teach her how to read the tracks of animals both big and small. Wolf, deer, marmot, mouse—she learned them all, but the hardest one came last.

"The most difficult creature to find," her father told her as he blindfolded her eyes and spun her in circles, "is the creature that knows all your tricks—and does not want to be found." Then he left her to count to one-hundred in the middle of the woods, his departure through it leaving no trace.

The forest was an open book to the Dragon Hunter, and he tutored her in its secret language. Here, this small burrow, almost invisible under the tangled roots of a great oak—this is a perfect spot for a young dragon to hide. The lake, over here, a pristine waterway untouched by humans—this is where the adult dragons come to nest, and mate, and feed. That empty corridor of sky, where the North wind howls into the South: their migration path. This dark, forbidding jut of rock against the mountainside, with its hollow, hungry maw—

"Don't ever venture into it," he told her sternly when she'd dallied at the mouth of the cave for a moment too long. "At least, not until the time is right."

"And how will I know when that is?"

But the Dragon Hunter was an enigmatic figure—by great cultivation on his own part—and would not say.

The lessons were continued indoors, too, for of the many secrets the Dragon Hunter kept, perhaps one of his most magnificent was what lay behind the small wooden door at the back of his cottage that led into the earthen hillside. The only person allowed beyond that threshold was himself, and eventually, Meralda, when she was old enough to understand that what lay within was much more perilous than anything that might lurk without. For behind that unassuming door was a vast network of caverns dug into the hillside containing the Dragon Hunter's personal library of ancient hidebound books, crafted from the strangest iridescent scales, gilded with gold, encrusted with rare jewels. The tomes sat on ragged wooden shelving that ran throughout the cavern system, and Meralda's favorite pastime soon became exploring the halls of books glittering under torchlight. To ensure her safety, the Dragon Hunter entrusted her with a golden compass. "A compass which always points to the heart of things," he'd told her, pressing it into her hand. With this gift, she was never lost in the cavernous library, for the compass always pointed to the heart of the study: the Dragon Hunter's desk built of solid mahogany, overrun by scrolls of ancient languages and sheaths of half-used parchment. The only clear space on the desk was a built-in side shelf used to display a family of little dragon figurines cut from precious stone. They were arranged in a line, first jade, then sapphire, ruby, and amethyst, and on afternoons when she did not have lessons, Meralda would sit in her father's chair, chin pillowed on hands, to watch the gems twinkle in the dim candlelight. When the light passed through them at the right angle, one could almost mistake the refraction for the rise and fall of a ribcage, a ripple of reptilian flesh; in these rare magical moments, she dreamed each dragon was alive.

So enamored was Meralda with the inner sanctum of the library, that she often forgot there was a world outside of it, but the outer world did not forget about her sisters. Each day they grew in grace, wit, and beauty, and each week when they ventured into town together, throngs of young men and women waited to meet them. Among the kludge that hung on Corvina's every word, there was one young man who listened harder than the others. He learned the art of her wordsmithing just as he had with metal, and on the day Corvina refused to tell any more stories but asked for one instead, he stepped forward and told a tale of his own. When he came to its end, the sparkle in her eyes was all the applause he could ever wish for. As for Dorata, among the gaggle of youth who chased at her heels, one boy pushed himself faster and faster until he could keep her pace. As they tied a race for the first time, his heart skipped a beat when she gifted him a new smile, meant for him and him alone. It was little time at all before Corvina and Dorata announced their courtships.

The only daughter who was not courted was Meralda. Though she could often hear her name whispered among the young townsfolk in the same reverent way they spoke of the Dragon Hunter, no one ever approached. In the beginning, this did not bother her very much, for she was quite young, and still the apple of her father's eye, but as her sister's courtships blossomed, and the eldest began to speak hopefully of marriage, Meralda pined for a suitor of her own.

"Oh, my heart," her father said, "one day, men will travel from across kingdoms to see you."

"Will they be handsome, like Corvina's blacksmith?"

"Yes, they will be very handsome," her father replied.

"And will they be strong, like Dorata's farmer?" And her father assured her that they would be. But she was not satisfied.

"And will they be brave, and kind, and loving, just as all the books and stories say?" At this, her father shook his head, accompanied by a deep, heavy sigh.

"My dearheart, they will be handsome, strong, and brave, for they will be knights of great valor and renown—though perhaps when they finally do arrive, you will no longer desire them."

Meralda could not fathom a situation in which this would happen; after all, knights were the dashing heroes of all the stories she'd read, in both the dusty, ill-kept town library and her father's own personal collection. But the Dragon Hunter sat her down and held her hands within his own.

"You will break many hearts, and many people will break your heart," he said, "but I shall tell you a secret: once your heart has been broken that first time—and provided you survive it — another such wound can never kill you."

Meralda was not greatly comforted by this proclamation; she was still dreaming of heroes and princes from faraway lands. To distract her, the Dragon Hunter fished an exotic trinket out of his Secret Armoire of Mysterious Curios, and she was satisfied for the day.

Her lessons were not, strictly, to hunt dragons; quite the opposite, in fact. The Dragon Hunter was a caretaker, rather than an actual hunter, and Meralda's tutelage reflected this— though not once, throughout all the lessons, did she ever glimpse a dragon. Nevertheless, the lessons continued, and she learned to hunt wild game while her sisters baked bread. When the midnight stars rose, and her sisters lay sleeping, she stayed up to chart the heavens, and record their secret dictates. But the most essential subject by far was that of languages. It is a widely known truth that dragons invented language, and taught it to humans only out of pity; as such, their mastery of the art is unparalleled. Meralda studied her father's ancient scrolls until she, too, became fluent in many dragon tongues, especially the language of riddles—but it was her sisters who, during the long drowsy summer afternoons, learned the language of love. And somewhere within the intervening years of lesson upon lesson, the Dragon Hunter grew old, and Meralda grew up.

***

Meralda had always known her father to flout conventions. Now, as she entered into young adulthood, she couldn't help but notice that sometimes her father's eccentricities dallied on the edges of madness. The riddles and rhymed couplets he once spoke in the privacy of his study, he now spouted publicly in the village market. He could often be found speaking to the vendors in verse, or languages long dead. Once Meralda even caught him trying to pay them with pieces of Fool's Gold; when she attempted to give him a purse of real coin in exchange for his pyrite, she was rebuffed.

"This is one of the highest forms of currency among dragons!" he insisted, dangling the offending sachet in front of her nose. "Second only to the currency of words!"

"And that might very well be true, but we are among humans right now," she hissed back, "and they will start to think you are a swindler, a thief, or worse—a fool!"

Her father deigned not to respond but looked upon her with such a grave stare of disappointment that she couldn't help feel a weight settle upon her heart. The Dragon Hunter turned from her and continued down the cobblestone street, his long cloak and multicolored scarf trailing behind him as he made his way out of town. Meralda scurried after her father, dodging the odd thrown tomato as she did so. Her eyes burnt at the humiliation but stayed achingly dry as the whispers and jeers of the townsfolk nipped at her heels all the way home. "It's the Dragon Hunter," they tittered, not nearly as reverent as in her youth—though perhaps they never had been, and Meralda had only wished it so.

Her father's new strange behavior was not relegated to the town; at home, he stayed locked in his study within the hollow hillside for days on end, roaming through the endless shelves and muttering to himself in a language that not even Meralda could interpret. He would emerge to fall ravenously on whatever his wife and daughters had prepared for dinner, only to disappear once more. The Dragon Hunter now refused to take his cloak off indoors; instead, he layered them one atop another and draped himself in excess scarves no matter the temperature or location. His walks through the wilderness grew more prolonged and frequent, stretching from early evening to the hour after midnight. Each time, Meralda watched him stride into the woods or across the empty plains until he was a black smudge on the horizon, and as the wind whipped up the layers of capes about him, he almost seemed to fly, skimming low to the ground on fabric wings. She kept vigil until her father dissolved into the landscape.

Meralda could never bring herself to be truly vexed about these new erratic habits; after all, they were but an amplification of the activities she and her father had always done together. Corvina and Dorata, however, had no such qualms. They would rib him good-naturedly when they thought him silly, and less good-naturedly when they found him embarrassing.

"One day, I'm going to go out for a walk and not come home," the Dragon Hunter warned them after one such incident. He held a long pipe clenched between his teeth and wore a heavy cape thrown over two other cloaks. As he prepared to go outside, Meralda thought she saw a flash of silver metal peeking out through all the layers of fabric—perhaps chain mail? The idea that he might need to wear such a thing twisted her stomach into knots, but before she could get a better look, her father covered up the odd material by donning a long striped scarf. His ensemble completed, he swept from the cottage for another impromptu evening sojourn.

"Humph." Her mother stood by the stove side, hands planted into hips. "He's been saying that for years now, but does he ever do it?" She clucked her tongue and returned to work, but when the Dragon Hunter did not return until the early dawn of next day, Meralda was not so certain, for already the smoke-scent of departure hung in the air.

Corvina was the first. She left her father's house to marry the blacksmith, who was enamored with her quick tongue and clever fingers. Another rotation of season's cycles and Dorata went to marry the farmer, who had long ago fallen for her deftness of foot and golden laughter. Soon, the only ones left in the cottage were the put-upon mother, the Dragon Hunter, and the youngest daughter.

"And is there no one who will love me for my quiet ways and my green, green eyes?" Meralda cried out one morning, throwing her spoon down into her porridge. Her sisters did not answer her, for they were having breakfast in their new homes with their new husbands. Her father could not answer her either, for he was absent, gone on one of his solitary quests. It was her mother who sat down next to her and assured her that one day, she would find her match.

"It won't be one of the village boys," Meralda declared. "They do nothing but speak ill of me."

"That's because they don't know what to think of you. Perhaps the man of your heart will come from farther afield," her mother suggested gently.

"I'm just the same as my sisters," Meralda insisted.

"Similar in many ways, yes," her mother agreed, "but they took more after me. You are your father's daughter, a creature of both wits and ferocity. There will be some who love you, but many more who fear you."

"Then perhaps I do not want to be my father's daughter," Meralda spat.

She regretted it as soon as she said it, but words were a fickle gift of the dragons, and once spoken, could not be taken back. She watched as her mother drew herself up to her full height of five feet. When the older woman spoke, her words were precise and cold.

"I journeyed far to meet your father, and I stayed because he was a good man," she said, "You are not made of the same mettle as your sisters, so do not expect the same ending to your story that they received. You will not get it."

Meralda felt her face crunch, and she bit her lip. Her mother's voice gentled into a soothing hush.

"Meralda, the mate of your soul must be your equal and opposite," she murmured, "for just as fire cannot fight fire, power cannot tame power. Only tenderness can do that, and it is a gift we call strength – but there are few men, or women, who know of this gift."

"Little wonder, then," Meralda muttered, "for this gift you speak of—it is foolishness."

"That is what it is to love a dragon."

"I'm no dragon."

Her mother said nothing else, returning to sweep the earthen cottage floor. Meralda exiled that conversation to the deepest caverns of her mind, and no longer spoke of love; her thoughts were consumed only by her continued effort to contain the emanation of chaos that was her father. When spring rains came, and the heavens rang with peels of thunder, Meralda followed him out into the storms. The Dragon Hunter brought a notebook, and his metal telescope, which threatened to char both father and daughter with a stray bolt of lightning at a moment's notice. They stayed in the torrential downpours until both were drenched through, the Dragon Hunter watching the sky and taking waterlogged notes while Meralda begged him to go inside.

"This is the mating dance of the dragons!" was his rebuff. "It lasts but one season every fifty years."

"Father, it's a thunderstorm. Nothing more and nothing less!" Meralda shouted, but she was drowned out by the tumult of the firmament. The Dragon Hunter continued scribbling notes in his saturated journal. Meralda shivered and kept watch.

When summer bled into autumn, the woods began to ring with gunshots, and the Dragon Hunter took up his rifle.

"There are men in the woods hunting after the flightless wyrms," he told her, his countenance unusually stoic.

"No, Father," Meralda replied, without any heart, "They're only poaching the forbidden bucks in the King's Wood." But he did not heed her and strode into the forest. Meralda waited at its edge all night for him to reemerge, too afraid to venture in after him.

In the dead of winter, the Dragon Hunter insisted on trekking out into the hinterlands of the forest to check on the young dragons during their first hibernation, despite the raging snowstorm and deathly temperatures. Meralda caught him by his sleeve at the door, pleading with him to reconsider. The Dragon Hunter embraced her with a tender smile.

"My dearheart," he said, "This is the life of a dragon hunter. Our foremost duty is to the dragons, even when it is dangerous. They must always be first in our hearts."

"But Father," Meralda whispered, "There are no dragons."

The Dragon Hunter's expression shuttered. His smile disappeared, a new sadness blooming within his eyes as he turned away from her. He went out despite the squall, and Meralda watched in disbelief as the blizzard seemed to part before him. Soon it had subsided entirely, leaving behind a virgin snowfall and a sky full of stars. Meralda went to bed in the comfort knowing that his journey would be a safe one.

But when dawn came, the Dragon Hunter had not returned. His youngest daughter waited by the door as the morning slipped by, watching the empty horizon.

"Oh, he's finally gone and done it then, has he?" Meralda's mother grumbled. She continued cooking, but Meralda saw the shine of silent tears running down her face. She watched their progress with fascinated dread.

When the sun reached its apex, Meralda could bear it no longer. Abandoning her post, she threw on her father's emerald green cape, took up his walking staff, and marched for the door, but at the last moment, she thought better of going out blind and made a detour to his study. A quick rifling through his notebooks and loose papers revealed no clues as to where he might have gone, and she almost left empty-handed. Then, through the clutter, a glimmer of old, familiar gold caught her eye: the compass she'd used so many times as a child. It sat half-hidden by a sheath of notes next to a little silver dragon figurine she'd never noticed before. She quickly slipped the dragon into the pocket of her cloak for luck and snatched up the compass, which she kept in a viselike grip until she stood outside at the start of her father's old trail. There, she held the precious metal up with open palms and pressed her lips to its glass face.

"Point me to my heart," she murmured, and the needle sprung to life.

The Dragon Hunter's tracks were easy to follow; he'd made no attempts to hide them, and the snow was fresh and unblemished. She followed his footsteps in loops and circles that flattened out into lines, and always the needle of the compass pointed true. She traveled over hill and dell, past frozen waterfalls and even the forbidden cave, and both compass and footprints led her still deeper, into the heart of the forest.

Until she reached the end of her father's trail.

There was no body. No sign of his presence. The footprints stopped mid-track as if he'd simply floated off his feet and into thin air.

She looked to her compass, but the needle spun round and round, without direction.

"Dragon Hunter!" she called out, and her cry rang through the silent wood.

"Father!" But she received no response.

"Dada," she whispered. The word died on her breath, a powerless summons that he did not obey.

Meralda combed the surrounding snow-laden woods for hide or hair of her father but found no trace. In the next several weeks, she branched out in all directions, to the same fruitless result, though she used every tracking skill she knew. But he was a creature that knew all her tricks – for he had taught them to her – and did not want to be found.

***

Winter reigned for months on end, but little by little spring reclaimed its strongholds of wisteria, rosebud, and tulip. All around their cottage, the meadows shook off their coats of snow, rivers of ice broke open, and Meralda marked down all the days her father remained gone. The tally stayed by her bedside, each strike an outlet for her silent grief.

In his absence, Meralda took up the mantle of Dragon Hunter and soon found that his legacy haunted her more than any ghost ever could. Whenever she went into town, the whisperings of the townsfolk caught in her ears; they still tittered among themselves, but now it was 'The Dragon Hunter's Daughter,' they muttered as she passed. Some of the more antagonistic villagers, who had hassled her father in his decline, now transferred their attentions to his successor. It was purely in her attempts to frighten them off that Meralda incidentally cultivated a mystique of her own.

Now when she visited the village, Meralda sang in dragon languages all the way there and back. She spoke to the animals she met, did sleight of hand tricks during transactions at the market, and sometimes, when she felt particularly impish, vanished herself in a flash of light and smoke from the middle of town. All this was more than enough to ward off the mobs that had stalked her father, but for those who proved more insistent, and continued to harass her, Meralda took to cornering them and posing them a riddle. Each wrong answer was accompanied by a brief electrical charge—but for the few that managed to guess correctly, Meralda rewarded them with a boon: perhaps a talisman, or a reading of their future. After such an encounter, said individual's fortune seemed to increase tenfold. Soon enough, many of the townsfolk vied for a chance to play Meralda's game of riddles, and while they could not understand her strange powers, they did at least respect her.

As amusing as the town could be, her real work lay beyond its borders. Each day she wore her father's green traveling cloak along with his walking staff or rifle. She tended the same trails and secret glens her father had been warden of, recording their natural phenomena. She tackled the study and the cavernous library, organizing the seas of papers as best she could. She read through her father's writings and even began adding to them herself. However, there remained one glaring obstacle in her conservation and academic efforts.

"I've still never seen a dragon," Meralda confided to her mother one evening, "My duty is to the dragons—Father said they must come first in my heart. How can that be possible when I've never even seen them?"

"I'm sure you will, when the time is right," her mother reassured.

"But how can you love something you cannot understand?"

Her mother clucked her tongue. "A creature may contain two conflicting impulses, just as a word may have two separate meanings. Your father taught you the language of riddles, did he not?" When Meralda sputtered in indignation, she chuckled. "This is a riddle you will have to solve by yourself, daughter-mine."

Unlike their mother, her sisters were not so understanding of this radical change within their youngest sibling. One or the other would often corner Meralda in town and beg her to give up her new duties, and while Meralda refused every time, they persisted throughout the spring and summer. Their plots culminated at the harvest festival, and when the trees shed their fiery leaves to reveal the truth of themselves, Meralda was ambushed by both of her sisters. They gripped her tight, one on each arm, and forced her to sit down with them by the feasting table.

"You'll never find what you're looking for by following in the footsteps of our father," Dorata warned, "or worse, you will, and you'll come to the same end."

"Little sister," Corvina chided, "you're not a small child anymore. Isn't it past time you put away the foolishness of an old man?"

Meralda looked between them both, the two shining beacons of her childhood, and for the first time saw a ragged hunger within them for the one thing they had never been given.

"I'm sorry," she told them softly, "but we don't have the same story. We'll never have the same ending." Then she wrestled herself from their hold and left.

And then, as though no time had passed at all, it was winter once more, and with it came the anniversary of the Dragon Hunter's disappearance. Meralda woke up that morning to a fresh snowfall, along with a strange itching in her bones that required her to jump out of bed, grab her best walking shoes and staff, and don her cloak.

"I'm going out to search one more time," she told her mother, who met her by the door.

"Meralda, do you not think I want your father to come home as dearly as you do?" her mother chastised, "But even I've accepted that you will not find him. You've looked in every possible place."

"Every place but one," Meralda replied, "and I think now the time is right."

She followed the path her father took, once more treading through unbroken snow as she headed through the forest. Eventually, young trees gave way to primordial old-growth, untouched by the men of the village, but as her father before her, Meralda knew each knot and root of every tree. She followed the memory of his trail until it veered further into the woods, away from the base of a high mountain, but Meralda stopped and turned to the cave nestled within the mountain's roots – the one place she had been told never to go.

The entrance was dry, but as she descended down into the earth, the air dampened as her vision darkened. She felt her way in further by following the cold tunnel walls with her hands until they fell away from her fingertips. Then she knew she stood within a vast cathedral of stone by the echo of her footsteps that ascended upwards into unfathomable heights. An unnatural wind swept through the empty hollow in even pulses, and she sensed more than saw the invisible movement of the dark.

"Hello?" she called up. At the ring of her voice, the heart of the mountain purred with carnivorous life. She looked up into the dark cavern to see two luminous moons—no, not moons. Eyes, white as the mists of morning and with the light of a thousand midnight stars, peered down at her from the blackness. She looked up into the face she could not see, of what could be—of what must be—a dragon. A rift of fire opened through the dark, and when the voice of the cavern spoke, it trembled the foundations of the world.

The scent of a daughter from the race of men has not graced our hall for some time. Tell us, Child, why have you come here?

"I'm searching for my father," she answered into the darkness. "He calls himself the Dragon Hunter."

His name is known to us, the voice rumbled, but we do not know yours. What is your name, Little One?

But Meralda had never forgotten a lesson, not even the first one.

"I'm the Dragon Hunter's daughter," she replied and planted her hands on her hips when she sensed the creature's amusement.

The one you seek is not here, the voice told her. You will never encounter him again in this life.

Meralda swallowed down her despair with a painful click of her throat. "Then...I'll go now," she stuttered, "and leave you to slumber in peace."

Ah, ah, the voice chuckled, for this information, and my time, I require payment.

"I have nothing of value to give you," she protested.

On the contrary, so long as you have your tongue, you possess the greatest treasure of all. The darkness shifted above her, and the voice was closer now, a sibilant hissing that slithered over the damp walls of the cave and into her flesh. I will pose you A Riddle, and you will have three chances to answer. A test, if you will, to see how much of your father's daughter you truly are. If you answer false, I will eat you whole.

"And if I answer true?"

...you shall receive a gift.

That sounded more like a threat than a boon to Meralda. Her frame trembled, and she slid her hands into the pockets of her cloak to hide the most obvious tremors; her right hand jolted in surprise when it met with a smooth stone in the abyss of fabric, and she closed her fingers around it for luck, the cool weight of it within her clenched fist giving her a semblance of courage. She squared her shoulders and jutted her chin, just as scalding breath and damp underground air conspired to make her shiver. The voice curled around her further in seductive sibilance.

Do you accept this offer?

"I do," she answered, sharp and clear, for she did not see any real alternative.

Very well then, the voice murmured, and then it whispered The Riddle into the shell of her ear.

The Dragon's Riddle was not unlike the kind her father used to quiz her on in her childhood: four lines long, separated into two rhymed couplets, with an added homonym to lead her astray. But words had not led Meralda astray for a long while, and buoyed by her lucky stone, her answer rang throughout the mountain hall.

She nailed it on her first try. All in all, it was a very easy riddle to answer—not because she thought the voice was trying to help her out, but because she knew dragons are prideful creatures, and not always as clever as they think themselves to be.

Hmm. The voice sounded perplexed. Have you heard this riddle before?

"No," she told it, "you just aren't very good at coming up with them."

The cavern shook with deep, molten laughter. You have the heart of a fool, the voice declared, and you will receive a gift to match. At those words, the skin of her left breast lit up in a sudden, painful fire, and she choked on a scream.

Go now, Little One, the voice commanded. Protect our kind as you would your own. She didn't need to be told twice, hurrying for the passage back to the outside world, the stench of burnt flesh left in her wake. As she ducked into the tunnel and scrambled for safety, she thought she heard one last unearthly rumble. Your father would be proud.

Meralda stumbled back through the tunnel in a daze of pain, emerging from the cavern to fling herself into the wood. She ran blindly through the trees until, at last, a misplaced step sent her careening to the ground. There she lay, panting wildly as snow soaked into her skirts, a puddle of terror and wonder. The gift from the dragon still burned. She ripped her clothes away from the wound, and her heart skipped a beat when she saw the green protrusion burnt into her flesh. She fumbled for her lucky stone to quell her panic—but, of course, it wasn't a stone at all.

A familiar silver dragon figurine sat in her palm, the very same one she'd discovered in the library a year ago before her first fruitless search. The little drake regarded her evenly as Meralda pressed a shaking hand to her lips. She looked from it to her mutilated skin and back again. Her eyes burned with an odd pressure. Her diaphragm seized as a foreign sound broke its way out of her, a wail built up from a thousand different hurts and hoarded in the hollow of her lungs, and then Meralda was crying for the first time in her life, drowning in an ocean of grief—and another, dearer emotion, that she still did not understand.

She cried for what seemed an age, but when Meralda finally wiped her nose, rose to her feet and brushed herself clean of snow, the stars still held their apex. Her steps were shaky, tentative, but she persisted, and soon the forest fell away into the snow-laden steppe and the empty, endless sky. The Dragon Hunter journeyed home through the winter bite with a single emerald dragon scale seared into the flesh above her heart. Tears burnt rivers into the crest of her frozen cheeks. When they caught on her tongue, she tasted love.

"I love you like salt."
King Lear in Respite Care, Margaret Atwood

A Test of Trouble

Catherine George

Catherine is an author of short speculative fiction.

When the baby is nine weeks old, Bree begins to suspect she is a time machine.

The evidence is this: it's 4:30 a.m. and Pippa is up for the third time, wailing. Beside Bree in bed, Max shifts and—accidentally, of course, she must have rolled onto his side of the mattress—elbows her in the back.

"C'mon, Bree," he mumbles. "If you can't get her to sleep, can't you at least keep her quiet?"

If only there were some way for Max to get more sleep, Bree thinks, settling into the rocking chair. More space in the town-house, better soundproofing—

"Or more time," she murmurs, to the greedy baby in her arms.

She closes her eyes. Opens them when the baby's warm mouth against her nipple falls away. The blinking red numbers on the clock say 2:15.

Time is untethered; the baby has untied it, released it to float up into the sky like a white balloon. It is 1:30 a.m. and Bree has either slept or she hasn't, one state or the other infinitely possible. Pippa lies quiet in the bassinet, barely visible in the orange slats of streetlight slicing through the nursery blinds.

Bree crouches over her and put lips to hair, tasting; nose to forehead, smelling. "Where are you taking me, little one?" she whispers. "When?"

***

In the morning Bree waits, eyes closed, for Max to grumble about her inability to get the baby to sleep through the night. He's right to be frustrated; he has so much on his plate at work. Tight timelines, investor pressure, so many people waiting to say he's wrong: *there's no economically sound way to get oil from stone.* Having a useless mess of a new mother stumbling around at home would try anyone's patience, let alone a man trying to melt rocks—

The sound of the shower slices through her thoughts. Over the falling water, she hears Max begin to warble a boy band tune—*I want it thaaa-at way*—and by the time he comes out, Bree has Pippa fed and breakfast ready.

Max throws an arm over her shoulders, still humming, and drops a kiss in her hair. He smells like the air before a rainstorm: earthy and metallic, riverine.

"What magic did you do in the night? he asks, sipping his coffee. "I feel like I slept for days."

This is her Max, Bree thinks, sinking against him: the Max who brings his friends over for dinner parties to show her off, like a diamond set in the shining band of his life, who leaves her sweet notes when he goes to work, listing his favorite parts of her body (*toes, tits, tip of your nose*); not the Max who slams doors, turns his face away when she comes to kiss him hello, who snaps "Not now, Bree!" when she knocks on his office door—

But that's all her fault, isn't it? He's tired of the chaos that remains of their once-perfect lives. Her perfume replaced with the fading scent of spit-up; milk stains on the leather couch; her body a bad taxidermy version of its former self, misshapen and lumpy.

"Maybe she's figuring it out," she ventures. "Sleeping, I mean."

He grabs a fried egg sandwich from the counter, spins her around and pulls her in for another kiss. "Whatever it is, keep it up."

***

She waits for Max to go to work before she calls Caro to explain her time machine theory.

"Aren't we all time machines, though?" Caro says. "Only the machine just keeps going forward."

In the distance, she can hear the sound of Caro's kids laughing, like flags fluttering in the wind. Bree can picture the big kitchen where Caro sits, the precise angle of the sun drifting through the white lace curtains, kids skidding over the wide pine board floors as they run through, the way she and Caro used to do.

"It's always like that with a newborn," Caro says. "Two months from now, time will be stable again. Speaking of, when's a good time for us to come meet her? Or for you to come out to the Island? It's been, what, four years? Since Mum's funeral. The kids would love to see their Aunty Bree."

"Oh, not for a bit," Bree murmurs. "We're just settling into a routine."

Something about Caro has always rubbed Max the wrong way—and, well, Bree gets it, Caro is Caro, loud, opinionated, always game for an argument. And maybe it's mutual distaste, at that; the morning of Bree's university graduation ceremony,

Caro had murmured, "You didn't tell me he was your prof when you started dating," disapproving, and Bree hadn't been able to find the words to explain that it hadn't been like that, he'd never lorded it over her, and besides she hadn't been a physics major or anything like that.

Since the wedding Bree's done her best to keep them apart, keep them from butting heads. Easy enough, with Caro on P.E.I. and Max and Bree in Vancouver.

"Well, let me know," Caro says, and Bree thinks, *I won't*, and turns to other topics, leaving things to lie unspoken in the vast span of kilometers between them.

***

By mid-afternoon, Bree has been to mommy-baby boot camp, done laundry and bought groceries, but somehow between struggling with Pippa's latch and getting her down for a nap, by 6:15 there's nothing more than a half-chopped potato to show for her efforts. Every noise outside the door sounds like Max's footsteps coming down the hall, heavy with disappointment that dinner isn't on the table. Again.

"It's a tough time for him right now," Bree says. Pippa stares back from the baby swing with unnervingly wide grey eyes. "With work, you know ..."

She remembers how excited she'd been, when she'd seen the two pink lines on the pregnancy test, how she'd imagined Max smiling down at the baby in his arms, ruffling his newborn's hair the way he'd ruffled Bree's on the day they met, in front of the entire first-year physics class. *A girl made of poetry*, he'd called Bree, that day, when she'd told him she was an English major. She had imagined him coming up with some sweet nickname for their child, too, murmuring it as he rocked her to sleep. But now, on the rare occasions when he holds the baby, it's as if he's holding a sack of potatoes, heavy and lifeless.

"He's right, it was probably a bad time to have a baby. If I only had more time ..."

Time: with more she could still be the perfect wife, and handle Pippa as well—no. Bree shakes her head to clear out the loose thoughts lying about in the fog of her brain. They're tripping hazards.

When she looks up at the clock again, it's only 4:30. There's ages left to get dinner on the table, so why is she worried?

When Max comes in he sniffs appreciatively. "Chicken cacciatore? Fantastic, I'm starving."

But even nine pounds of time machine can't hold her world together. A week later, Max comes home and finds her with a red-faced, inconsolable Pippa shrieking in her arms, broken dishes all over the kitchen from the pile she knocked off the counter while trying to find a clean soother.

"God, Bree, I don't know why I thought you'd be able to manage all this," Max sighs, waving a hand at Pippa, the kitchen.

"Sorry," Bree murmurs, grabbing the broom. Pippa calms in the sling, soft head lolling sleepily against Bree's chest, as she sweeps. The broken plates reassemble as hills of shattered pottery in the dustpan. "My fault."

Max slumps onto the couch. "Yeah, well. You're not the only one falling down on the job. Four months until the investor demonstration, and nobody's hitting their targets. Sludge! We're producing fucking sludge, not oil."

"What's the problem?" She doesn't understand the process he's developing, not really, beyond the basics reported in the news (*a laser-shock technique for converting the kerogen in oil shale into synthetic crude without the need for surface retorting ...shock waves cause the kerogen to liquefy ...will open vast oil shale fields to drilling at $20 a barrel*), but she can still listen.

"An issue with the wavelength. If we could just..." She tries to listen, but Pippa starts to grizzle again, little hiccups of baby despair. Bree bounces, patting her rhythmically, trying the little *shush, shush, shush* that had worked so well for a few days and now doesn't seem to do anything.

Max smacks a hand against the glossy leather of the couch. "I'm sorry, Bree, I know, I'm boring you. It is boring, you're right, I can see how you'd rather be anywhere else ..."

"No! No, I was listening, I just ..."

"You think about the baby too much," he mutters, then sighs. "It doesn't matter, anyway. The real problem is we just don't have enough time."

***

Bree gives Max more time: time in his office at home, hours repeating while he's focused on the screen, and time on his motorcycle on those long solo rides where he does his best thinking, snaking up the coast past Squamish or out into the Valley. She slows time down, speeds it up. Smooths over the sour mood that comes when Max has to wait for things by cutting out the hours that come between. "That went fast," he says, suddenly cheerful again.

She wonders what happens to the rest of the world as the clock repeats, when time seems to roll in reverse. Does the whole world add ten thousand seconds to the weight of their lives? Or is it just the three of them, Bree and Max and Pippa, blown off in a bubble of time all their own, popping and collapsing back into the pool of the world when they catch up again?

Max might know, but when she asks about time travel and paradoxes, he laughs and asks if she's been reading too much science fiction.

***

The day of the investor demonstration Max comes home early, quiet and brooding. After Pippa goes to bed, he presses Bree to her knees in front of the couch, drops his jeans. When she's done, he leans back and releases his rough grip on her hair, letting her slump to the carpet below him.

The words seem stuck in her throat, but she needs to know, she can't try to fix whatever's broken if she doesn't, so she coughs it out.

"How was the investor demonstration?"

He laughs bitterly. "Fantastic, if you like explosions. Leah typed in the wrong fucking numbers and left a mound of smoking ash in the middle of the floor. So now the investors think we're going to blow a crater the size of an airplane hangar in the shale deposits."

"Is it—is it something you can fix?"

"I can fire Leah so she can't put her slippery fingers all over the wrong fucking keys again, and then try to convince everyone it was a one-off."

Leah Zhang had been at the team dinner they'd hosted the night before; as the only woman on Max's team of physicists, Bree had always liked Leah enormously, but Max had told her that it would be awkward if she was friends with his employees, so their contact is limited to the monthly meals and running into each other at the gym, waving across treadmills.

Last night Leah had come into the kitchen to tell Bree she had a soy allergy.

"It's not deadly or anything," she'd said. "Just bad hives for a couple of days."

It's the work of a moment to send a note back to herself: *mix tofu with the ricotta; don't tell anyone.* It helps to think it might save Leah's job—

Time wobbles. Tips.

Bree catches herself daydreaming, mind wandering while she feeds Pippa pureed banana. Max is still sleeping off his night of celebration. When he'd stumbled in late last night, cheerful with vodka, he'd swept her into bed, touched her gently, gently, the way she likes it.

"The investor thing went well?" she'd asked, after.

"Perfect," he'd said, fingers tangling lazily in her hair. "Perfect."

***

The next morning, Bree lies with Pippa on a picnic blanket at the park, spring undoing the small deaths of winter. She lifts Pippa into the sunlight arcing through the leaves overhead.

"You see?" Bree murmurs, and Pippa giggles, kicks like she's swimming in air. "He was always so nice, before. It's—this is just a work thing. It'll pass."

The life she'd imagined for them is still in reach, just around time's bend. Manipulate time enough, and she can turn them back to the way things were meant to be …

A memory stirs: eight years ago, before they'd left Ottawa, lying in the grass beside the canal. Aspens overhead, sunlight glinting off the water, flat and still as the summer air; she is dappled with light, drenched in green. She'd spent hours reading poetry (*Time is a test of trouble/But not a remedy*), listening to the distant clunk of the locks rising and lowering. A perfect day, at least until she'd gone back to Max's apartment—he'd told her she had to move in, save her money—and found him waiting, silent, at the kitchen counter, phone in hand.

What's wrong, she'd asked, and he showed her the screen: twenty attempts to call her, no answer. She'd laughed, shakily. *I forgot to charge it, sorry. I was down at the canal reading poetry.*

After that she always kept her phone charged, never went out without telling Max where she was going. Stopped talking to certain friends, the ones Max accused her of going out with that day. She stopped reading Emily Dickinson in the sunshine. And Max didn't leave her.

Memory is a time machine, too, Bree thinks.

***

She interferes, again and again. Time wobbles. And sometimes tips—

—Bree rocks Pippa to sleep, bleary eyes registering shadows on the nursery walls. There are shadows everywhere these days. At the park, phantom children run past. When she turns there's nothing but branches, waving in the wind.

—he needs more time. And time is something she understands now —

"I didn't know she could do that," Max says, watching Pippa sign *more*, take the bit of apple Bree is holding out. "Did you teach her that?" For once he looks entranced with his own daughter, as if she's a science experiment that's borne out his hypothesis, until he learns forward and—

—looking in the mirror at the purple watercolor bruises on her back and wondering when that started, how much of it is the baby carrier digging in, how much is something else.

Some days it feels like she's fallen into quicksand, a place where time gets sloppy. On the phone with Caro she can't remember when they last spoke. Or are they not speaking? The phone is in her hand, numbers undialed.

"You sound tired," Caro says. "Everything okay?"

The mirrors and motor housings arrive early from the factory, their journey sped up.

Max smiles and smiles and takes Bree hiking, throws her into the summer-warm lake and comes barreling in after to pull her close against him in the water.

"Isn't this nice?" he murmurs. "Just you and I, for once."

—she finds time to read poetry again, to a squealing and clapping Pippa: "But now, all ignorant of the length/of time's uncertain wing ..."

What does it take to change the world, Bree wonders? Do these changes only wobble, time righting itself like Pippa rising to her feet and finding, in a moment, her balance? Or are they like delayed reactions, explosions only sounding—

—they rise as one in the pews, Max somber in black, while a woman who looks like an older version of Leah begins the eulogy. Pippa stirs and Bree shushes her. A freak accident, that's what they're calling it, but Bree wonders if the electrical fault in the laser system has her hands on it, if Leah was torn apart more by the manipulations of time than the manipulation of reality. She will bend time again, and undo—

"Are you alright?" Leah asks, from the next treadmill over. "You've been looking tired lately."

"Pippa's keeping me up," she says, obscurely happy to see Leah. "How's work?"

"Could be worse. We're making headway, but there's an issue with the design of the laser housing—the metal alloy we're using is too brittle to—well, you don't want to hear about that, right? You get enough of that at home ..."

A metal-alloy test can travel back in time. It can shudder the timeline, rip it sideways—

"Are you alright?" Leah asks, feet drumming a rhythm into the treadmill. "You're looking beat."

"Pippa's teething. How's work?"

"Oh, pretty good. Never enough time ..."

She understands time, now. She swims in it, sticky as an afterbirth.

She takes Pippa to the library. Pippa lifts a board book over her head, like a hat.

"I like your hat, love," Bree murmurs. This is funny. Pippa begins to turn the pages, but backwards: unwinding time. It's hard to say if this is memory, or the here-and-now, and what the difference is. When Bree looks up the sky is starlight, a day lost to time's voracious appetite—

Outside a cabin in the Gatineaus, starlight on snow, breath crackling, in nothing but a slip and sneakers. *You can come back in when you're sorry*, Max had said. Sorry for what? She can't remember. Maybe she never knew. Snow begins to fall, then suspends, flakes unmoving—

—she wakes in the rocking chair, baby on lap, heavy-limbed, warm, like the comfortable weight of a cat in her lap.

***

Leah says things are going well, better than last week, better than last month. But Max doesn't smile when he comes through the door at night, doesn't kiss her hello. His footsteps as he paces in the den sound like explosions. Bree always seem to be sweeping up something he's broken. She starts wearing long-sleeved shirts.

***

"Yuppie fools, driving around in SUVs and claiming we should turn our backs on oil," Max mutters, when the news shows protestors outside the gates at his lab. Their signs sport calls to protect the aquifers, pictures of oil-drenched frogs and lynxes: *make love, not lasers.*

"Why are they worried?" Bree asks. "Isn't there a containment field?"

"Nothing's perfect. Some leeching into the water table is probably inevitable." He looks up, catches her frowning. "What did you expect, Bree? We're increasing access to fossil fuels. It's not a wind farm."

"I guess I thought ..." she says, but trails off when she sees his too-bright eyes trained on her like a laser.

"What? What did you think?"

"Nothing. I didn't think anything."

"What, you think you're better?" Max stands up, slams off the nearest light, then another, one after the other, until the house is dark. Pippa in her high chair begins to cry. "How's this, Bree? Are we saving the world yet?"

Yes, she thinks. She had thought she was saving a world: her own, remaking the happy family she'd dreamed of. But maybe there's no way to save the world, in the end.

***

Sludge, it's only sludge, that's the word in the industry, whispers growing that the last hope of Big Oil is just a physics professor high on his own theories. The investors are pulling out, exploring other avenues—

"I have the key now," Max yells, smacking his office wall. "They won't listen. Just a shift in the wavelength, but they can't see it."

Bree steals a printout of his solution. Six months should be long enough—

***

"Hi, love," Max murmurs, coming up behind her as she dangles a glass over the open dishwasher. His hands snake around her and he begins to sway, humming a love song. She puts the glass down and leans her head back against his collarbone.

"How's it feel? To have it done?"

"Fantastic," he says, pulling her into the living room and spinning her around. "Glorious. I don't know what I'll do with all the free time. Dance with my wife, I guess."

She laughs and nestles against him. "I like that plan."

"Who were you talking to at the celebration yesterday?" Max murmurs, lips beside her ear.

"Yesterday?" she says. "Everyone, I guess. Everyone?"

"Oh, really?" Suddenly he is too close, hands on her hips freezing her in place. "Flirting with everybody, were you?"

"No, Max. I wasn't—" Her hips feel like an implosion, crashing in under the slow squeeze of his palms. He smells like the air before a storm: charged, explosive.

Bree imagines herself as a performing bear, dancing in response to his every jerk on the leash. Trotting out the same phrases, the same ducked head, penitent eyes.

"I'm sorry. I won't do it again."

***

Max paces the living room, taking calls from reporters, headhunters, the team at the test site with questions.

Bree tries to keep Pippa quiet, but she wants to play with blocks, to yell with joy and surprise when a tower wobbles, crashes to the ground. Max puts up with it for ten minutes, for twenty, then steps on a wooden block in bare feet, and Bree only gets there by the skin of the moment, her hip in the space where Pippa's head was, taking the blow.

"Clean up after her, why don't you?" Max says, short.

***

On the narrow, shaded path between the allotment garden plots, Pippa lectures the plants in some tongue only she knows. *Lu lu lu ba ga lumdo*, she says, shaking one little hand, dictatorial. She pauses in her tirade to press the tip of a stick into the sandy soil at the edge of the blanket, working it back and forth until she has created a small mound, and then unleashes another long string of syllables.

Bree wonders what a universal translator would make of Pippa's baby babble. Somehow it would find a way to reduce the glorious nonsense of Bree's chatter to awkward syntax, bad grammar. All of Pippa's world is in there: a poetics, a dream-manual, a language with only one speaker. A language she'll only know for a few more months, before it's slowly overwritten by English, and the tongue-of-Pippa will become a dead language. Maybe she'll dream in it for a few more years.

Or maybe she'll dream of time, swirling and coalescing around her.

Maybe she'll dream of Max.

Bree doesn't, anymore; the firefly pinpricks of the life she'd imagined have faded, gone dark. They weren't real, anyway. Just dreams, dreams that would never have come true, no matter how long or far she chased them through the universe.

No, she thinks. Pippa won't dream of Max, either.

Bree leans forward, hugs Pippa close, whispers a date, a time, a place: September 17, 2015. The day she saw two pink lines on the test, and knew someone was growing inside her. She hadn't told Max right away, clutching the news to herself, joy growing along with the child. When she finally told him, he—

No, that isn't right. Where did that thought come from? She'd never had a chance to tell him, never let him know she was carrying his child. Now she regrets waiting, but how could she have known? If she'd known, she would have told him not to go out on his motorcycle that day, not to drive up towards Whistler, to the place where he inexplicably missed the curve, drove off the road and into the rock face. *We don't know what happened*, the police inspector had said, hat in hand, a tentative hand on her shaking shoulder. *He didn't even try to swerve. It was like the corner came up on him too fast—we don't know. We just don't know.*

Bree shifts in the rocking swing on the big back porch, looking down the valley towards the fields where the potato plants run like a green thread through the rusty blanket of soil. Somewhere beyond, just out of sight, the sea. Caro's boys are playing out behind the house, their joyful cries ringing out against the vault of the sky. Thank God for Caro, for taking her in two years ago— pregnant, unemployed, widowed.

At the bottom of the stairs Pippa wobbles along the grass towards the dahlias, laughing as she reaches for imaginary butterflies.

If only Max were here to see this, Bree thinks. He would have been such a good father.

Inspector 36

Kristin Hooker

Kristin Hooker is the author of Idiots and Robots.

Inspector 36 stood across from, and alongside, long rows of Somebots inspecting garments. Are the buttons all there? Are there threads hanging off?

Her name was Chantelle, but her lanyard merely said, "Inspector 36," and she was the only flesh and blood person in the entire warehouse at the moment. The bots, a quarter of which, by law, had to represent a real person receiving a real paycheck, were almost silent. The fabric of the clothes shushed over their plastic and metal appendages.

Chantelle chose to wear soft leather gloves during work because repeatedly passing her hands over the fabrics dried them out. They'd been a Christmas gift from her mother.

The bots were relentless. They inspected three garments each in the time it took Chantelle to inspect one. The flesh and blood people were free to work in person whenever they wanted, but few did. Chantelle was different. The work made Chantelle feel good. She liked the satisfaction of looking at a stack of perfectly folded shirts that she'd folded with her own hands. Shirts that would all be worn by someone. Maybe someone on the other side of the world. The bots were no better at folding than she was. They were just faster.

Every so often an employee would check in remotely. A small green light would appear and signal that someone was on the other side of a screen "seeing" you, but you couldn't see them. Usually, the ones who checked in were new employees who felt like they should be doing something, when the truth was that the head office preferred employees be involved as little as possible.

"Hey, what's up, 36?" a woman's voice asked.

The green light shone on the bot across from her. Chantelle rolled her eyes with little subtlety. "Nothing much. How are you?"

"I'm good, but hey, what was your name again? Charlotte? Crystal?"

"Chantelle," she said.

"We've only spoken once before. I'll remember now. Chantelle."

"And your name is...?"

"Kelly."

"And what are you up to today, Kelly?" Chantelle asked. She yanked an earbud out of one ear to be polite. Kelly was interrupting the audiobook Chantelle was listening to called *The Power of Presence: A life unplugged*.

"Oh, just sitting at home, eating some cheese crackers, and watching a series called *Gentleman's Fancy*. It's about a brothel and all the people who come into it. Scandals and all that. You should check it out! You'll be addicted!"

"I'll have to remember that," Chantelle said, trying to keep the extreme disinterest out of her voice, and failing.

"Hey can I ask you something?"

"You can ask. We'll see if I answer."

Chantelle filled a crate with exactly fifty folded shirts, set it on a conveyor belt behind her, and returned with a crate of uninspected shirts. She wished Kelly would leave, and was not the least bit curious about what Kelly wanted to ask.

"Why don't you rent a bot to work for you?"

Chantelle sighed. The new hires always asked this question. "I like coming in to work. It gives me a sense of accomplishment. It gives me some time alone," she said, same script as always.

"But don't you want to stay home with your kids?"

"How do you know I have kids?" Chantelle asked, feeling unsettled by Kelly's nosy question.

"That was presumptuous. I was just guessing. I apologize."

Chantelle straightened and picked up speed as much as she could. She cleared her throat and perked up her voice. "I have two boys. There's nothing wrong with a mother working outside the home."

"Do the rental fees bother you? What if the rent on a Somebot was a little less expensive?"

"It's not about the fee entirely. I like working. But I *am* glad not to pay for bot rental. It's like, half a paycheck. It's too much. We need that money at home."

"Ask her about child care," came a man's voice in the background.

"Shut up, Steve," Kelly whispered. "Sorry, my husband thinks I'm hogging all the crackers. Men! So anyway, do you pay for childcare while you're at work? Wouldn't you save money by staying home with your kids instead of shelling out money for a sitter?"

"I don't pay a sitter. We live with my parents. Grandma takes care of the kids."

"Oh."

Kelly went silent. Chantelle hoped it was over. She knew Kelly was a corporate spy; some rich bitch. *Who are they fooling? They think I'm stupid,* she thought. *They think working class people are stupid. They wish I wasn't here. They wish I wasn't human. They'd fire me if they could. Cheese crackers my ass. They're probably sipping froufrou coffee and thinking of ways to screw us over even more.*

Chantelle could see from the corner of her eye that the green light was still on. She kept on inspecting and folding shirts with the little green eye staring at her. Chantelle lifted her earbud to her ear to re-insert it, but was interrupted by Kelly again.

"Chantelle, did you realize that while we were talking, you forgot to put your inspector sticker on one of the shirts?"

A blast of panic struck Chantelle's heart and she struggled to keep it inside. Any feeling that she was superior to Kelly by virtue of being a decent person evaporated.

"Oh shit," Chantelle said. She flipped through the stack and found the shirt. She affixed a number 36.

"Do you make a lot of mistakes like that?" Kelly asked.

Chantelle's heart sped up and her face turned red with shame. She needed this job. She even liked this job.

"No, I don't usually make mistakes," she said, trying to keep her voice calm, "but you're sort of distracting me."

Kelly's bot hadn't stopped inspecting, folding, and labeling shirts at all during their conversation. The world of the warehouse kept spinning with no one to witness or care about Chantelle's distress.

"Sorry to distract you," Kelly said. "I was just curious. You're an odd woman. Or, not odd, unique, I suppose. It's almost risky to work. Here at home with my cheese crackers and my TV, I never get injured, never make mistakes. I couldn't possibly get fired. It's a pretty good system having bots do all the work."

"I guess so," Chantelle said.

"And kids grow up so fast. Enjoy them, Chantelle. And maybe kick back and enjoy *Gentleman's Fancy*."

"I'll think about it."

"Have a nice day."

"You too," Chantelle said.

Her heart slowed. She put an earbud back in her ear. Her gloves felt damp with sweat. The green light kept watching.

Maeve in the Picture

Clare McNamee-Annett

Clare McNamee-Annett is a writer in
Surrey, British Columbia.

"So, what, is she your girlfriend?"

Maeve can hear his voice in the antechamber despite the closed door, the double-paned glass, and the insulated walls. His breath stinks—she knows by the way Cara wrinkles her nose—and when she tastes the residual sour in Cara's mouth, Maeve shudders. Old beef. She glances over her shoulder and looks through the glass. He's a big man, dressed in his paramedic uniform like the rest of the gathered crowd. He has a yellow smear on his left breast pocket. *What's his name...Huxley? Anderson?* Maeve always forgets Cara's coworkers. She'll call him Mustard. Maeve sees Cara shoot Mustard a look that would turn blood into ice, then turn back to the training room. *Ok...they are not on good terms. Noted.*

Maeve feels a sudden pressure in her chest. She can't tell if the pressure is from Cara's nerves or her own, but she knows everything is riding on her performance. There are two full-grown pigs in front of her: a pink boar with a tattered ear, and a larger sow with a black spot across her back, both guzzling oats from plastic buckets. The select group of assembled paramedics has assigned Maeve to the sow. Maeve tries to engender some empathy. But the pressure on her chest just gets worse.

"Ready?" says a voice over the intercom. *Female...must be Wilson...or Schwartz.* "The shooters are getting into position."

The whole room smells of the pigs' stench, wet oats, and mud, but Maeve's nerves are keyed up now: Maeve can smell the sow's distinct scent. Earthy, bitter. Raw. She has no curiosity as to the flavor. Pigs are similar to humans, their thinking goes. Similar weight, total blood volume. Their livers filter blood just as fast.

Pigs aren't the weirdest creatures to have been inside this precinct, according to Cara. But there is a reason the cameras are off, and the shutters are closed.

"Yes. I'm ready." Maeve tries to sound like she means it. Two rifles poke through a slot in the glass. It doesn't matter if one shooter misses and hits her instead: Maeve already has enough *creeahqua* in her bloodstream to kill a rhinoceros. *A dart to the throat. Lucky pigs. Cleaner than teeth.* Maeve pushes down the memory before her chest begins to seize. She rubs the sheath she's gripping in both hands. Rubber talisman. She grits her teeth.

It is three o'clock in the morning, and Maeve must slap this sheath to the sow, suck her blood faster than the 1.8 milliliters of active *creeahqua*, administered by dart, can Turn her into the swine equivalent of a bloodsucking monster.

Which is what I am. I am a bloodsucking monster.

Maeve reminds herself every day.

Her competitors are Randy Aston, the best paramedic in the precinct, and the DiaBlue 3600, the fastest blood dialysis kit on the world market. The DiaBlue 3600 waits beside the smaller hog, its suction ports primed and ready. It is a squat, black, portable machine, with sleek sides and fat clear plastic tubes running up and down its middle. A machine. *This is what they want me to be*. Maeve doubts she will ever convince them.

Cara passed her paramedic qualifier's exam last month: she studied for six weeks, it was all she ever talked about, so Maeve can tell you the specs of every blood dialysis kit in circulation. If you ask her. Not that anyone *would* ask her. Her own father doesn't speak to her, anymore.

There is only one DiaBlue 3600 in all of Lincoln County. It is property of the Six-Five, the central branch. The Four-Eight— where Cara works, wherein Maeve now stands, waiting for two darts to hit two full-grown hogs—has it on loan. For "training purposes." *Ha!* The Four-Eight's ambulances are stocked with DiaBlue 800s, Maeve knows— ten years out of date because the whole fanging industry is underfunded —*what a boon for public health*. Neither kit has prevented a victim from Turning. But the 3600s filter blood at three times the rate of the 800s. They're the best shot any paramedic has to save a life, after a vampire assault.

Sure, the DiaBlue 3600s are fast. But Maeve is faster.

And yes, I am her girlfriend, Mustard Stain.

***

Maeve dreams she is at the beach with Cara. It is high noon. For a moment, the full sun above her head makes it too bright to see anything. But then, her eyes adjust. Her father, Lionel Shapiro, is serving peach cobbler in a glass Tupperware. Cara turns cartwheels at the shoreline.

Lionel puts down the knife. He picks up his camera.

"Maeve! Get in the picture, too!"

"I don't want my picture taken." It's a lie. Maeve wants her picture taken more than anything, but the photograph will show a vacant space where her body is supposed to be, and Maeve can't bear to watch her father see it.

Cara runs up behind Maeve, grabs her waist, wrestles her into the shot.

"No—please." Maeve feels the words leave her mouth, like something released, something with wings. But her feet are pulled, magnet-like, through the sand. Soon she is feet from the tide.

"Sweetheart." Lionel puts his camera down. "You'll want to remember this day."

Cara flips herself onto both hands. Lionel takes the shot, and the flash goes off. It's an instant Polaroid, so there's the ritual shaking—"Don't get sand on it, Cara!"—and, then! *What? It's impossible! How is it possible?*

Maeve is in the picture.

The image has emerged on the photoreactive square: Cara in a handstand, covered in sand; Maeve, holding Cara's knee, mid-laugh. Her head is thrown back. Her mouth is wide open. Lionel has captured the moment just before Cara falls.

Maeve stares at herself in wonder. *Am I ever this happy?* But of course, it's in a photograph. She has to be.

There is a moment before she wakes when Maeve forgets what she is. Her chest rises by habit, then falls of its own accord. Her throat is dry—she sleeps with her mouth open—and when she closes it, her mouthguard feels heavy, tastes sour.

Mouthguard! Teeth! Vampire.

Her eyes snap open. Something rattles in her chest. Her breathing weakens until she lies on her back as still as stone.

She can taste everything in this house. There are so many flavors on the air: paper, dust, sugar, chamomile, cologne, cinnamon, and coffee. Noises rush in like a flood. She has too much knowledge, with sudden clarity: there are racoons in the park two streets down; there is a murder of crows overhead; a car door opens, three streets away.

Maeve hates everything about herself. Especially when she dreams about her Pa.

Maeve's father, Lionel Shapiro, bakes the best fruit cobblers. He bakes peach, apple, pear, blackberry, blueberry, raspberry, strawberry, and rhubarb cobblers in a six-inch circular ceramic pan that is worn rough and black around its edges. When Maeve was a child, Lionel baked a cobbler every morning before leaving for the public library, where he worked the late-morning-till-evening shift, five days a week. Every afternoon when Maeve arrived home from school, the cobbler would be waiting on the counter with a note. *Love you, kiddo. Eat your vegetables first. Wash your hands. Practice piano. Pizza's in the freezer.*

It was always just Maeve and her father.

He was right to cut ties. Who wants a vampire for a daughter? I'm a sick creep, I'm a sick fanging creep, thinks Maeve.

Maeve tries breathing again. She tries to calm down. She's so hungry. She's so fangdamn hungry. She stretches her chest. She sucks in cubic liters of air. The air goes willingly, but then it sits there, dead and stale. She releases it. She smells the cavity of her lungs as it escapes.

She hardly recognizes her own scent anymore. She tries breathing again. Faster, this time. Maeve gulps down three breaths in a row. *Maybe the feeling will come back.*

But air is a foreign body. It just isn't the same.

She looks around. She is lying on an old single mattress with a spring jammed into her side. It's night. It's dark outside. The restless hour just past curfew, when streets are quiet and crickets chirp from the gully behind the old house.

The bookstore café, *Crosses and Carafes,* spans the two floors below. Maeve worked as a barista here. Before she Turned. The benevolent proprietor, David March—Maeve's old friend—still lets Maeve work nights. She shelves and sorts merchandise for the price of her room and some cash. So, she lives in this attic, with the overstock books and whatever new shipment has arrived.

Cardboard boxes are stacked on three sides of the old wood room, labelled in black marker. *Vampire Literature, Defense Guidebooks, Self-Help, Poetry from the Damned.* There's a single window above the mattress, which Maeve has covered with a heavy wool blanket. It's drafty. A single pane of glass. Drooping floorboards. Maeve doesn't feel the cold, but Cara says *it's fanging colder than a ghoul's tit.* So Maeve has bought a space heater, which collects dust under her desk table.

Leering at Maeve in the center of the room is a large, pale blue ceramic lamp. The lamp is broken at its base, missing a hand's width gouge. It leans, south of Maeve's mattress, at a thirty-five degree tilt. There are seventeen black-and-white photographs of this lamp, taken at strange angles, hanging with clothespins from a string along the back wall. The photographs are dry, now. If Cara sees them, she'll say *what the hell?* Or, *are you fanging kidding me?* The lamp saved her life. Cara doesn't like to remember. So, Maeve unpins the photographs and places each into the drawer of her desk table. They add to the eight-inch stacked pile. *Self-Portraits,* Maeve calls them.

She rolls the wool blanket, opens the window, and climbs outside.

Night air tastes like pollen, cut grass, and wet metal. Then alcohol, electricity, and gasoline. Then the tar from the rooftop tiles. Then pine sap, roadkill, spilled coffee, old grease, burnt rubber. Maeve climbs to the top of the roof. She lies on her back under a weathervane. A drip of water collects at its lowest point. Each drip hits her forehead, then dribbles to the base of her neck in tingling little rivulets she imagines must feel cold.

She breathes again, tries to make it feel natural. She'd take up smoking if it wasn't an expensive habit. Anything to ease her nerves.

Maeve hears Cara's car door *slam!* a full twelve minutes drive away. She tracks her girlfriend's progress with the old sedan's various sounds. It's a countdown. She hasn't eaten in twenty-four hours. She takes inventory. The sheath is a folded wedge under her pillow. The stopwatch is perched on her desk table. Yes, she put the photographs away, why have another row?

At last, Cara's Aveo pulls onto the shoulder of the residential street below. Cara runs to the café's front door. The lock *clicks* open. She is inside the old bookstore café in twelve seconds flat. Maeve is counting.

Being a paramedic, Cara is permitted to be out past curfew. But it's dangerous—*so fanging dangerous,* Maeve pushes the memory down—so, Cara has the car-to-door-entry routine down to its minimal risk, even though the whole block is alarmed.

Now that she is inside the building, Cara moves slower. Maeve can hear each footstep, *thump-thump-thumping* up the stairs.

Maeve swings back through the window, closes it, pulls the wool blanket into place. The door creaks. "It's fanging colder than a ghoul's tit." Maeve snorts and plugs in the space heater. The electricity *snaps,* then it *whirrs* hot air into the dusty attic. Cara drops her bag in the corner. "Hi."

"Hi."

Cara steps over the lamp with a scowl that says *why do you keep it?* Old pain and exasperation. But the lamp is a constant reminder, for Maeve. She refuses to throw it away.

Cara sticks the rubber sheath to her neck. A thrill shoots up Maeve's spine. With a sudden and incapacitating urgency, Maeve is hungry. This hunger is practiced. Pavlovian. It isn't real, she tells herself. *It isn't real. I'm a trained dog, I'm a trained bloodsucking dog.*

How can a demon be hungry? Hunger is for the living. Maeve isn't alive.

Cara sets the stopwatch to twelve seconds. Which means thirty-six milliliters of blood, give or take.

But blood is rich, and wet, and tastes like a million metallic scents, and Maeve dissociates as she bends her head, as she bites the sheath and pierces Cara's neck, and sucks Cara's blood up through it. *Creeahqua* gets stuck at its borders, she knows: the sheath sterilizes her teeth. It blocks Maeve's poison and prevents Cara from Turning.

I almost Turned her, I almost Turned her, I almost fanging Turned her. Whenever Maeve and Cara are this close, and whenever they are touching, Maeve can't push down the memory of how *fanging close* she once came.

Maeve's guilt doesn't stop her from drinking. Hard gulps, pure force, as fast as she can. Cara's *gasps* are no more than odd rituals, these days. Rituals. Strange but necessary. Just like everything else in Maeve's life. Maeve is haunting the living. Maeve is on borrowed time.

The stopwatch *beeps*. Cara rips off the sheath; Maeve pulls herself away. She feels Cara's hand on her chest, firm pressure on her sternum. Cautious barrier. Ineffective. Just a warning. Like a sharp word, keeping her at a distance.

Engage, take what you need, step away.

She forces her feet back. She takes two steps. She stares out at the blue ceramic lamp. Its broken base calms her by inculcating the familiar cadence self-loathing.

Cara takes one shaking breath that she tries to smother with the palm of her hand, but it remains the loudest thing in this room. Maeve hears it. Cara sits down on the mattress. She wipes the sheath with hand sanitizer and a rag. Her motions are mechanical. Maeve frowns.

"Are you okay?"

"Yeah." Cara keeps her head down. Maeve doesn't believe her. None of this is enough. It's not enough blood; it's not enough touch. But it's what Maeve can count on. With a sudden, painful passion, Maeve hates every part of it. How long can they do this? For the rest of her life?

"If I was rich, I could buy blood from the CDC."

"Stop," says Cara, looking up.

"It hurts you," says Maeve."

"We've been over this. It doesn't hurt too much. I can take the pain."

Maeve sits down, her right knee brushing Cara's left. "You shouldn't have to, Cara."

Something tells Maeve she is starting a fight. Because she doesn't want to show up, tonight. Because she doesn't want to meet Cara's coworkers and be tested, be laughed at, be scrutinized.

"Can you stop feeling shit about yourself? I agreed to this. It's my responsibility."

"But it shouldn't be."

Cara scowls. Maeve hears the change in her heartbeat. *Thud-thud-thud-thud-a-thud.* "What are you saying?"

I'm saying I'm a fangdamn mess. Maeve says: "I wish I was better for you."

"You're good for me." Cara's eyes flash in the lamplight. "Can't you see that?"

Stop lying. Maeve looks away. Why does Cara keep telling herself that? *I'm a bloodsucking monster. I'm not good for anyone.* "Cara. You still have blood on your neck."

"Oh, whatever!" Cara wipes the blood with her sleeve. It's no mystery she's angry. Maeve has broken their code. Cara picks up her bag and stalks to the door.

Maeve stomach drops. "You're not going to sleep here tonight? The trial is in six hours."

"Yeah. I know what fanging time it is." Cara opens the door. "I'll see you at the precinct."

Maeve shakes her head. She glares at the ceiling as the attic door slams. She could yell *Cara! Wait!* She could catch up in a heartbeat, dash down the stairs. Apologize, self-deprecate. Get down on both knees. Is that what Cara wants?

Maeve's body feels heavy. She can't muster the energy. Maybe it's good that Cara is angry. *We haven't touched in six weeks. Except feeds. Maybe we'll get to a breaking point. Maybe we'll just stop pretending.*

Maeve takes out her Yashica Rangefinder. She opens the hatch and adds a new cartridge of 35mm film. Her last. She sits down beside the broken lamp. She points the camera lens at her face. *Click. Click. Click. Click. Click.* Maeve scowls into the shutter as it flies open and shut. Then she bares her teeth. Then she flips it the bird; then she sticks out her tongue. Then she mimes a scream.

***

Maeve leaves the attic at quarter to three. Her worn sheath is clutched in her hand. Security blanket. She runs. She catches up with Cara's car around Bayou and Jasper and jogs beside the old grey Aveo. Cara is blasting the radio—"In recent news, the White House has issued Cease and Desist orders to 'Armageddon Blood Right'...the CDC is tightening their legal requirements for registered supernaturals." She checks her blind spots. She scowls at the road. Her passenger window is open a crack: Cara opens it to defog the windshield, and always forgets to pull it closed. Maeve smiles, despite herself. Her mood has improved since the feed. She tastes salt, vinegar, potato starch from the residual air on Cara's tongue. Chips in the glove compartment, she guesses.

Cara's car picks up speed. Maeve runs faster. Air pushes back against her chest, buffeting her. Maeve's face and arms tingle.

Night is bitter cold, she assumes. Cara doesn't look out the window, but Maeve knows, when jogging at fifty clicks, her vampiric form is a slip of wind and shadow. She doubts Cara would see her. She feels invisible, but not like in a photograph. In a guardian angel, unseen-yet-tethered sort of way. Besides. Maeve likes to run. It isn't the worst thing, she concedes.

She can tell Cara is still angry by the way her heart pounds in her chest, by the rate of her breathing, by the way the air around her smells like anxious sweat, and how she pushes a tape into her tape deck with too much force, and how she doesn't nod her head when "Like a Moonwalker" begins to play.

Cara is counting on me.

Everything will ride on Maeve's performance. The fact that she is even welcome at the paramedic precinct is a godforsaken miracle, but Wilson is a moderate and Schwartz trained in public health, and Jeffers-the-anti-vamp-radical was fired. And fang it, Cara vouched for her. Cara found the sheath. Cara fed Maeve, when she was days away from (a second, more permanent) death. This is all Cara's idea. There's a new pressure in Maeve's chest, now. She doesn't want to be here. She can see the illuminated red roof, the sign, "Paranormal Medic Precinct 48," at the end of the road.

She isn't going to let Cara down. Not after everything she's done to her.

Will she be able to save a pig? With her teeth and her repressed bloodlust and her insidious hunger...Can she save a victim from her fate? Is it even possible?

***

Maeve is already mid-run when the dart hits the sow's left jowl.

She reaches the animal before its squeal peals across the room in a wet scream, checks the dart cannister (empty), pulls it, throws it across the room.

The sow flings her head. Squeals, again, with the sting.

Maeve jump back. Stands by. Guarding; cautious. *This stinging is going to get worse, unless we do this. Like cold fire in your veins. Is that what you want?*

The sow returns to the oats at hand, but she's nervous, now. There's a sick tension in her haunches Maeve can't help but see. Maeve's heart wrenches. *Did I shake like that?* She swallows something in her throat that tastes like bile.

She moves behind the oat bucket. She slaps the sheath over the sow's puncture wound with supernatural speed and fastidious precision. She imagines, to the paramedics in the window, her arms are a vague blur on the air.

She smells Randy burst through the door before she sees him. Deodorant, sweat, adrenaline, that burnt-metallic taste of nerves. He runs to the boar, grabs the suctions ports, and jams them into the boar's seeping puncture wound. The poisoned blood at the boar's neck is extracted, transfused. The sleek machine hums. The boar hasn't even flinched.

Did they sedate him? Fanging cheaters.

Rage focuses Maeve's jittery nerves. She looks down.

Her sheath looks wrong on the sow. Only Cara has worn it, before this moment, and there's something grotesque about the way the rubber covers the sow's hairy skin, catching in the bright lights overhead. The way it ripples. The sow looks so vulnerable, now. Her head is shaking, back and forth, as if trying to swat bees at her neck. *Creeahqua* is running up her veins. Maeve has to work fast. She doesn't want to. But this is a test. *Only a test.*

Who else might wear the sheath, in the future?

Some human. Some human dumb enough to get bitten.

Self-loathing overwhelms Maeve. She uses it. She lunges down.

She puts two hands on the sow's front haunches, pushing her to the ground. She could force the pig down—she can lift a car, she's done it before—but the sow gives in. Like she knows.

Firm pressure, Maeve tells herself. Don't spook her. *Engage, take what you need, step away.*

Maeve puts her mouth to the rubber. It feels so fangdamn wrong. Unsettling. She draws out the blood. *It's snake venom,* Maeve tells herself. *It's venom. Just venom. Humans do this too.*

The sow is bleating, now.

Pig's blood has a particular flavor, something akin to young grass and tar. Maeve gulps the poisoned blood and memories flood her. After she Turned, before Cara found the sheath, Maeve survived off a half-liter of pig's blood from the butcher, twice a month. It was never enough. She was sick every day. She tries to feel grateful for the additional meal, but the taste just makes her nauseous. Her nerves feel electric. Fangdamn it, she needs to calm down.

Maeve watches the sow. Her whole body is shaking. But she's bleating less, now. That's good. The *creeahqua*—the heaviness of it, the distinct, bitter pitch—tastes dilute. Almost gone. Maeve doesn't want to be here, drinking this blood. She closes her eyes. She hears voices.

"Bite load is gone from Pig B. That's under three minutes, Wilson."

"Two minutes *ten*. Fanging hell. Is the machine broken?"

"It's perfect. It's scanning Pig A without a hitch. Randy's only siphoned off thirty-six percent."

"I told you! A bloodsucker is faster than dialysis. It's what they're made for. Why haven't we *thought* of this before?"

"Don't call her that."

"I'm sorry?"

"You heard me, Jacobi. Her name is Shapiro."

"Stop! Look at Randy!"

"Something's wrong."

Maeve smells the cascade reaction overpowering the boar's blood. She can smell it before Randy sees the symptoms—"Run," she shouts, to Randy. "Run." Then, his wide-eyed terror. Sweat beading up his brow. The quaking; the ramrod-straight limbs; the high-pitched *squeal*.

Randy's scream is pure terror. He drops the tubing and runs. No mystery why. It is said cross-species transfer has a Turn rate of 1 in 10. The best dialysis kit in the world: not fast enough. The boar has Turned, anyway.

He makes it out the door. There's a siren overhead. "Get out," says the voice on the intercom. *Get out.* But she's a bloodsucker, too. What does it matter? There's a sow beside her, with a still-beating heart. Have they all forgotten?

Maeve pulls the sheath from the sow's neck as the boar runs at the sow. *Poor sow, lying on the ground.* She's in a dream state. The boar lunges. What uncanny speed. She throws herself in its path. She grabs the boar at the throat. She wrestles the animal to the ground. His body is a squirming, rearing, crazed mound of fat, muscle, dirty flesh. Then there's a shot from the window. A piercing *squeal.* Another shot. There's blood everywhere. The boar goes slack beneath Maeve's body. The pressure in Maeve's chest explodes.

She sees her body convulsing with sobs from a vantage point a few feet above her own head. She's on her knees. Maeve can't cry, there are no tears, but this is as close as she can come to it and it's a violent, painful approximation. Her shoulders shake. Her chest is heaving. Her throat emits strangled sounds.

The sow's squealing and the siren fade into a dull *hum,* but Maeve hears Cara's voice behind the glass, cutting through it all. "Fang it, let me in there!"

"Are you crazy? It isn't safe."

"*Let me in the room,* Wilson! Let me in the goddam room!"

"Oh, the boar's out cold! Just let her through!" Mustard pushes his weight against the door. Cara sprints inside. Now, the vampiric boar—what's left of him—is splayed across the concrete floor. He's bleeding from the head wounds. The sow, shrieking, runs full speed in tight circles around the room. *Shtick,* another shot. The sow bowls over, too.

"Breathe, Maeve. Breathe."

"I can't." Maeve's chest feels physically constrained. She can't open her lungs. Her skin is on fire.

"Maeve, look at me." Cara's hand presses hard on her sternum.

"Breathe, Maeve." This pressure, outside her, pressing inward; this perfect, painful constancy. "You can do anything."

***

"There's pig hair on the sheath." Maeve lifts it, like an apology.

"We'll wash it." Cara swallows. "You did it. You did so well."

"I need to leave. I need air. Are we done?"

Cara looks confused. *Does she expect me to be happy?* There's blood everywhere. There's blood on her face, Maeve can smell it.

"I'll tell Wilson we're leaving, okay?" says Cara. "I'll drive you home."

Maeve nods.

When she leaves the room, she feels pressure release. She smells old wood, the day-old sweat on dank clothes of the precinct—spilled soup, pen ink, a bleach-based cleaning product—and these smells are ten million times better than the smell of death in the training room. She grabs her sweater from a bench. She wipes her face. She sees the sweater smeared with boar's blood. *Another dead bloodsucker.* These paramedics are heartless and cruel.

They part as Maeve walks past. They stare shamelessly as she picks up her things. Somebody murmurs, "well done". When Maeve reaches the door, she hears: "Shit, that was nuts. I've never seen one move, before."

She steps outside. Fresh air on her skin. It isn't hard to breathe, out here. Open air is better than that trapped, suffusive hell. Why can't people see that?

At least the the sow is alive. She thinks it, bitterly.

She waits by the car. She stares into the night.

***

"Who was the man who let you in?" If Maeve talks first, Cara might think she's okay. "The big guy. With the mustard stain. It was good of him."

"Andrews." Cara drops her bag in the back seat. She looks at Maeve as she buckles her seatbelt. "He really came through in there."

It was dangerous of you. The boar was still moving. How could you? Maeve doesn't say it.

"I was worried about you, Maeve. You freaked out." Cara turns on the ignition and starts to drive. It's four o'clock and the roads are empty. Cara's A19 curfew clearance badge swings from the rearview mirror. The mirror that only sees Cara.

Maeve doesn't say anything.

"Are you going to talk to me about it? Are we going to drive home in silence?"

Cara's voice is rising, now. Maybe she's angry because she's scared. Cara is often one or the other. Fear and anger are stalwart companions. Maeve can never tell them apart. "I just...I don't know what to say."

"You proved you can do what our *best* equipment can't, Maeve. You can save a victim from Turning, after an attack. You can draw out the poison fast enough. Even with the sheath." Cara looks at Maeve. Maeve keeps her face blank. "God, should I be pushing for this? Do you even *want* to save people?"

"I'm going to screw it up." *Even tone*, Maeve tells herself. *Level voice. That's the key.* "You know I will."

"Why would I think that? Why would you say that?"

"I almost Turned you." Maeve's voice is too loud, but the words are out of her mouth. There's no retrieving them. "Before we found the sheath. When I was living off pigs' blood. From the butcher. Remember? If David hadn't heard you scream. *Fang it,* Cara. If David hadn't come running..." *If he hadn't knocked me out with the blue ceramic lamp.* "I was so *close* to it, Cara. Don't you care? You'd be dead right now. You'd be hunger-crazed. You'd be searching for your next fanging meal."

"You were starving." Cara's voice is quiet. "You weren't yourself."

"How do you know what I am?" Maeve is almost shouting. Why doesn't Cara understand? "How can you *trust* me to be around all those *people*? Your colleagues, Cara. Schwatz, Wilson, Andrews. How can you even be in this car with me? You don't love me anymore, you just...feed me. I'm a burden. Why don't you just leave?"

"You're spiraling, Maeve."

"I'm not spiraling! You're the one with the problem! I'm a bloodsucker, Cara. How do you even trust me?"

Cara pulls the car to the side of the road, pressing the brake. They decelerate with a slow deliberateness that seems too thought-out to be emotional. *Forty clicks. Thirty. Twenty. Nine. Five.* The Aveo stops. Gravel crunches beneath the wheels.

"I do trust you. I've trusted you from the minute I first saw you, serving coffee. I trusted you after you Turned. I know it's naïve.

I'm a fangdamn trusting person. But it's true. You're going to have to live with it."

"I'm a monster, Cara."

"I've known you long enough to know what you are." Cara glares. The ferocity in Cara's expression takes Maeve aback. She rarely sees Cara this angry. "What? I should hate you as much as you hate yourself? Is that what you want?"

Maeve looks at the floor. They haven't talked about this before. "Didn't it...hurt? Weren't you terrified?"

"Yeah." Cara takes a breath. "Yeah, Maeve. I was terrified."

"I can't forgive myself," says Maeve. "I just can't. Ok?"

"I wish things were different," says Cara.

Break up with me, leave me, save yourself, Cara. But Cara looks up. Cara is still here, watching Maeve. Maybe she doesn't want to leave, but how can she sacrifice her time, her blood, her youth...and for what? For Maeve? God, is Maeve worth it? After everything?

"I wish things were different, too." Maeve says it, miserably.

They sit in the silence, and the night feels heavy. Anything could be outside this car. Maeve believes, for a moment, that this is the only place she has ever been: sitting, with Cara, in a car on the roadside. The two of them, in the silence. Losing heat.

"All I've ever wanted to do is to save people," Cara says. "I don't understand why this is a hard decision for you."

"I'm not like you, Cara. I don't want to save people." It sounds so selfish, admitting it. Cara is such a selfless person. What Maeve wants feels trivial in comparison. But she says it, anyway: "I just want to show up in a picture."

"What do you mean?"

"I just...I want to see my face again." Maeve's voice cracks. Fangdamn throat, she can still taste the pig. She closes her eyes. She smells the car and everything in it. She smells the mucus in Cara's sinus, mixed up with the salt from waiting tears. She wishes she still had tears. "I don't know who I am, anymore. I don't know what I look like, now." If she says it, the words will be outside of her. Isn't that a good thing? What else can she do with them? "Sometimes I can't even remember my own face, Cara. God, I miss my Pa."

Cara takes a long breath. She wipes her mouth with one hand. She is thinking. "Look. I don't know how to make you see yourself, Maeve. I wish I could. But...you know, I see your face, every day. I promise you: you're not a monster. You're just a girl. Okay?"

Maeve doesn't know how to believe this, so she just takes Cara's hand. The pressure of Cara's palm feels like something akin to warmth. It doesn't tingle like the night air: it feels constant. If Maeve closes her eyes, she can almost imagine they're sitting in *Crosses and Carafes*, in the chairs behind the Geography section, in full daylight, surrounded by people. She can almost believe she's alive, again. Like she was, once. When Cara first touched her.

"Hey." Cara's voice is gentle. "You should call him."

***

"Hello, this is the voicemail of Lionel Shapiro." A 'beep' sounds, and Maeve presses the phone to her ear. She takes a breath of air.

"Pa, it's Maeve. We haven't spoken in a while. I understand if you don't want to see me. I understand if you hate me. Or if this is too painful." *God knows I've been hating myself too.* "I...just wanted you to know that I'm...still here.

"You gave me a funeral. It was a nice one. I watched from the vestry. The lilies were perfect. You gave the most touching eulogy. I never knew you kept the Christmas card I made in sixth grade that began 'felicitations, father.' I didn't know it made you laugh like that. Fangs, I was such a strange child.

"I guess that I'm a strange adult, too. I take pictures of lamps. I spend all my money on film, photosensitive paper, and fixation chemicals. But I'm still here, okay?" *I didn't starve on the streets. I didn't kill anyone.* "I have an opportunity, now. To save victims. Like me. I can stop them from Turning, after being bitten. At least, it seems like I can. I'm faster than the paramedics' dialysis equipment. In Lincoln County. They want to take a chance on me. It's a risk, and...fang it, every bigot this side of Sycamore is going to have an opinion. But I'm going to try, Pa." *You sacrificed so much of your life to raise me.* "Maybe I can save some other Pa's kid. From the same fate. If you catch my meaning." *I want you to be proud of me. Even though I'm...something different, now.*

"I know it's not your fault I was bitten." Maeve stops talking. The insistent, urgent memory presses on her chest. It's trying to crush her. A sudden *wham*; riptide force. Her back, on the concrete ground. Cold sweat-gooseflesh prickles up Maeve's skin. She has to keep talking, or she'll never get this out.

"You couldn't pick me up from work that night. I knew that. I made the choice to walk home. It could've happened to anyone. You couldn't have known. I needed somebody to blame. It wasn't fair I said those things to you, Pa. I'm so sorry."

I miss you. You always took such good care of me. You always cared. Maeve takes another breath. Air is foreign body, but for this moment, it is hers.

"Cara's well. She'd love to taste another one of your cobblers, sometime. You know she always did love the peach ones." *I miss you, Pa.* "I hope you aren't lonely. I hope you've...been keeping well."

Maeve presses on the telephone switch. The dial tone *beeps,* reminding Maeve of her feeding stopwatch. *Engage, take what you need, step away.* She replaces the receiver. She takes a step back. She doesn't know if her Pa will hear it. She doesn't know if anything will change. But at least the words are out there. As least Maeve has tried.

***

"I want a tight run, alright?" says Wilson. "Efficiency and speed. Who knows what could be possible, tonight? But I'll say this: in all my years as a paramedic, this is the first night I've *ever* believed that we might have the chance to save a victim from Turning. I never thought this day would come. So, whatever happens just...give it your best shot. Okay?"

A cheer rings out through the precinct. The paramedics gathered are giving Maeve the side-eye. Cautious, tentative looks. There's excitement in this room. Everyone is buzzing. But there are hushed whispers, too, when she's close. Nervous laughter, like she's easy to spook. Rumors fly.

Maeve is dressed in black, with red neon stripes up the side of her pants, and a GPS tracker under her skin. It's not how the paramedics dress, but Maeve is the DiaBlue on the team. Why complicate things? She is just their machine. The GPS tracker forms a small ridge under her wrist. It smells like newly soldered metal. It makes Maeve feel exposed. How can a machine trace her when she can't even see her own face? Life is full of these jagged little ironies. At least Cara is here. At least Cara is coming with her. She climbs into the ambulance. She sits down in the back of the van. She grips the clean-again sheath in both hands.

"This is it," says Cara. "No more drills."

Cara is nervous. Maeve feels it, in the pit of her stomach. Cara's nerves feel like Maeve has swallowed something alive, and it's bounding around inside her gut. But she smiles at Cara. This is a big day. Maeve embraces her nerves.

The ambulance pulls out of the precinct parking lot. Maeve hears the throng of anti-vamp protesters before she sees them. "Die, vampire! Starve them out!" Their voices are raucous, unbridled. Vicious. Filled with hate. When the ambulance passes the chain-link fence beyond the Four-Eight, protest signs come into view. "Hear No Evil, See No Evil" catches Maeve's eye. Chanting cuts through the walls of the ambulance. "Die, fangs! Starve them out!" Their terror smells like puke and Maeve feels infected.

"Do you think you can do this?" says Cara. Her eyes narrow. Her heart races, Maeve can hear it. Cara knows what is at stake. If Maeve is employed, she's legitimized. If she saves victims from attacks, she is a hero. She debunks those anti-vamp slogans; she upends their campaigns.

"Bloodsucker! Starve the Fangers Out! Die in a Gutter!" Maeve imagines attacking the throng. How long would it take to bite every protester? To Turn them into the monsters they hate? *Three minutes, tops? Maybe four.* But staring at the signs, Maeve realizes it doesn't hurt as much as she thought it would. If anything, seeing the words on display—actually reading them—feels like a strange relief.

"Devil Incarnate! Vampire scum." They aren't in her head, anymore: they're outside of her. They're somebody else's words, now.

Maeve takes Cara's hand. She squeezes it. "I've been told I can do anything."

Cosmic Resolution

Hannah Hulbert

Hannah Hulbert is an author from the south coast of England. She has two children, a husband and an affinity for goblin culture.

The tentacles are trying to get in through my bedroom windows again. Their shadows wriggle behind the net curtain. The occasional slapping sound reminds me they're still there when I hide under the duvet. I think they're knocking—trying to attract my attention. But without any bones that wet splat is the best they can manage. I wonder what a monster could want with a kid like me, but my train of thought is almost more terrible than the tentacles.

I screw my eyes shut and will them to go away. There's a long slurping and a rattle of glass as a sucker attaches by accident then pulls itself free. I wish our landlord had installed the double-glazing he promised when we moved in two years ago, or that it wasn't just us two in the flat. I'm only a kid and Mum is...Mum. What can either of us do about it? Why're they here, tapping on our window on the third floor, anyway? I shake my head, as if I can shake away the thought of it. There's a lull in the knocking, and I tell myself that it's my willpower that sent them away, but I'm not fooled by the lie.

Last time they came, I told Mum. That was the third time I'd noticed them. It took me ages to build up the courage to slide out of my bed and knock on her bedroom door. To point out the shadows waving at us through the backlit curtain. To make the whole thing real by speaking it out loud. I braced for her mocking me, but she didn't. I wish she had. She just blew smoke and told me to go to bed. I thought then that she didn't believe me and that had been hard. But now, thinking back on it, I realise that she did, and that's even harder.

And so I don't run to tell her. The TV's loud through my bedroom wall, and I probably won't be able to get to sleep anyway. She's watching a late-night chat-show, and all I can make out is swearing, followed by Mum's drunken cackle. She only laughs like that at someone worse off than her. I don't hear it often.

But then there's a smashing in the kitchen and I go rigid. The TV's now talking to itself and the tentacles are gone from my window. If anything, that's worse. My mind jumps to a conclusion and I force myself out of bed to investigate.

I shuffle across the room, wrapping my duvet around my shoulders, the world's most pathetic armour. It's the same set I've had since I was five, with the Happy Farmyard Friends on. I was so excited when Mum bought it, and she beamed down at my happy face. Last year she promised me a more grown-up one for Christmas. And again for my birthday a couple of months ago. I picture that five-year-old and her smiling mother until a clattering from the kitchen and footsteps in the hall yank me back into the present.

The bulk of the duvet wedges me in the doorway. There's Mum in the hall, fag hanging off her lip and a can of lager in one hand. In the other, she's clutching a baseball bat. She looks ridiculous. The thought of either of us playing any kind of sport is a joke.

"Go back to bed, Marina," she slurs, and stumbles towards the kitchen.

The door's ajar and the only light comes from a street lamp shining in through the window. It's dark, but shadows meander all over the beige lino inside. Mum pulls the door closed with a click. It has a knob rather than a handle. Landlord was supposed to replace those too, but I'm glad he hasn't bothered.

We stand staring at the shut door for a while. Every now and then there's a smash, followed by the tinkling of something trailing through shards of broken crockery. I tell myself that if the tentacles wanted or were able to get out, they would've by now. Another lie I don't believe.

After a while, Mum turns round. The light that makes it in through my bedroom window catches on the silver scar running from her temple down to her jaw. The fag's burned down to a stub at the end of a cylinder of ash. It's impressive the whole thing hasn't crumbled yet. Any moment now it will, and Mum will swear about it ruining her sweatshirt, already singed in a dozen places.

"What're you doing there?" she says, as though I'm the most surprising thing in the flat. "Thought I told you to go back to bed?"

"Is it safe?" I ask. Then, once the floodgate's open, the questions rush out. "What was that? What's it doing here? What does it want? Shouldn't we *do* something?"

"Buggered if I know," she shrugs.

"But...it was real? I mean, I didn't imagine it?"

"Just go to sleep, girl. It'll be gone in the morning."

"How do you know that?" I narrow my eyes at her. "What's going on? Why aren't you freaking out about this? Mum, this isn't normal!"

She snorts. It might be a laugh. The column of ash collapses, and she curses flamboyantly as she brushes it off herself. Then she stubs the butt out on the wall and shuffles back to the TV, which is still flickering and shouting to itself in the dark. She closes her bedroom door, sealing herself off from the rest of the universe. I stare at the yellowing paintwork, wishing she would tell me what's going on, but at the same time wishing it wasn't going on at all.

The clattering, squishing tentacle sounds are still coming from inside the kitchen. I reverse into my room and close the door, moving my bedside table in front of it, just in case. Then I lie on the mattress, still wrapped in my duvet like a pod. I can't hear the kitchen over the TV and Mum laughing that horrible laugh, but the sound rings round my skull. I know it's still there, whatever it is, and I can't stop thinking about it.

***

The sunlight glows red inside my eyelids, warming my face. I must've fallen asleep. The world is soft and fuzzy, and so's my memory. I hatch out of my duvet egg and haul the bedside table away from the door to open it. The kitchen is hazy with smoke. Mum's knelt beside the freezer, rifling around for something. I go to the bathroom.

After I'm done, I check the kitchen. Mum's leaning against the counter-top with a cigarette and a stale doughnut she salvaged from work yesterday. The freezer's shut and the floor's clear. She's swept the wreckage into a mound under the little folding table and duct-taped corrugated card over the broken window-pane. I head to the kettle and boil it.

"Could you make us a cuppa while you're at it? There's a good girl," Mum says, as though last night never happened. She crams the last of the doughnut into her mouth and sugar sticks to her red lips like moths on flypaper.

"Last night..." I start, staring at the cardboard patch, but there aren't any words big enough to contain all I want to say.

"Leave it, Marina. You know I'm not going to talk about it. And help yourself to doughnuts." She strides out of the room wreathed in fumes.

I push down my seething frustration and make two teas in the cleanest mugs I find. My brain's buzzing with questions that no one will answer. Mum only ever brushes them aside and I'd lose the precarious friendships I've made at school if I started talking about tentacle monsters. The rest of our family is yet another unanswered question. It's just me and Mum, two islands in an ocean of chaos. I take the last doughnut and my tea to my room and get ready for school.

When I come back to the kitchen, the only sign of Mum is her mug, teabag abandoned at the bottom like a shopping trolley in a pond, and a wisp of smoke coiling from the ashtray. I check the bread bin to make myself a packed lunch but the last of the loaf is sprouting turquoise spots. The fridge isn't any better. Mum must've been checking on a stash of something good in the freezer. I open the door and root around, hoping to find a secret supply of sausage rolls.

I'm fishing around behind the frozen peas and boxes of unidentifiable leftovers when my fingers brush against something smooth and soft. I empty the compartment, piling icy packages round my knees, until I've made a big enough gap to extract the mystery item.

It's a book.

Under a glittering layer of frost, a thick, black-leathered tome rests in my hands. Alien letters embossed in gold on the front make my eyes water if I look at them too long. My hands tremble, and not just from the cold. When I flick through the pages, my stomach contorts and my ears throb with my hammering pulse. The words are in English, I think, but my eyes glide over them without absorbing any, like a sheen of oil. The middle pages flop open to reveal a set of black and white lithographs.

They're old and dark. The caption underneath reads: "The Elder Gods." I lean closer and try to make out what they're supposed to be. A jungle full of creepers or the overgrown ruins of a city perhaps? I lift the glossy page up to my face. Or maybe waves, as tall as skyscrapers? Beneath them, almost moving under all that cross-hatching, is something tentacular. I jerk my head back, as though to stop myself diving into that inky sea. Then, heart pounding, I bury the book away again behind softening bags of veg.

I drop the carrier bag full of broken plates and glass into the bin in the alley behind the flat on my way to the bus stop. We're only a couple of streets in from the docks, and the air always smells of fish. You can just glimpse the sea from Mum's bedroom window, but down here all you get is the stench and the noise of seagulls. The bus stop's a five-minute walk and the bus is due in ten, so I poke round the alley a bit for clues that might explain what the tentacles were up to. Nothing.

The bus is full of people on their way to work and elderly couples doing whatever elderly people get up early on a weekday to do. Everything is so *normal* I can barely stand it. All these people living their bland lives while my mind bulges with questions. Those pictures rise and fall in my memory, making me nauseous.

And even though it makes me queasy, I can't shake them out of my imagination, like they're hooked in.

That book must be Mum's. How else could it have got into our freezer? So she must know what that monster is. Maybe she even knows why it's tapping on my window. She's a dragon hoarding a great trove of answers. The old lady next to me keeps shooting me Looks so I try to focus on something else and stop grinding my teeth, but I keep drifting back. I can't decide whether it's reassuring that I didn't imagine the whole thing or not. I can't work out what's making me more furious, the monster or Mum.

At school I keep my head down, pretend everything's normal, and avoid conflict. That could be my motto. I try to concentrate on my exercise book, but the lines wriggle hypnotically. That evening, too exhausted to hold it in any longer, I avoid Mum after she gets in from work. If I don't see her, she can't lie to me and I won't explode in rage. I add the book to the bonfire of unsolved mysteries at the back of my mind and try to ignore it looming there, begging for a spark.

Mum's got two slices of quiche, a bag of wilted salad, and some jacket potatoes that've been kept warm for the last 24 hours wrapped in foil. We microwave what we want on individual plates in silence and then take our meals to eat separately in our rooms. I have chemistry to do for tomorrow. Mum has the second part of a murder mystery to watch. There's a lot of screaming, but at least she isn't laughing tonight.

Around ten, the tentacles come back. I pretend I don't notice, as if I can carry on working while they're there, slurping around outside. I could hand in the assignment a day late. I never ask for extensions, so Dr. Plough would probably cut me some slack. I try to focus on the molecular models of hydrocarbons in the textbook and not the damp patting at the glass.

But then I jump at the sudden ripping, screeching, tearing sound on the other side of the wall, and I think with a sinking dread of the kitchen window. By the time I'm in the hallway, Mum's already there with her fag in her mouth and her baseball bat in her fist. The kitchen door's wide open and we've left the light on. The tentacles writhe in through the broken glass, over the sink and out across the floor, dark and oozing and rough. And *real*. Horrifyingly, unquestionably real. I open my mouth, expecting to scream. Instead, a strangling noise comes out and I collapse sideways into the wall and slide down onto the carpet.

There are four tentacles. One has massive hooks at the end and has snagged on a cupboard. It's trying to drag itself free, splitting the plastic off the plywood. The others grope around as though they're looking for something. Mum steps in quick, bat raised, and slams the door before they get any closer. She turns to me and makes eye contact. There's no shrugging this off. I'd challenge her if I had a voice, but it seems to've done a runner. I don't blame it. I'd scarper too if my legs hadn't turned to jelly.

"Well," Mum says. "Seems you and I need to have a little chat." She swings the bat to rest on her shoulder as though she's been fighting zombies and leads me into her room. I struggle to my feet and follow.

I'm not usually allowed in here. Everything's stained a dirty yellow. She switches off the TV with a remote she digs out from under a heap of underwear and moves her plate of leftover dinner off the bed to make space for me.

"Mum, what's going on?" I ask.

She sighs theatrically and lights a fag from the butt of the previous one.

"Well, kid. I guess it's time we had 'the talk.'"

I scoot onto the bed and fold my legs underneath myself. At the other end of the hall, something pounds at the door with a squelching effect. Mum's already halfway down the cigarette, sucking at it like a nicotine vampire.

"What d'you know about the Elder Gods?" she asks.

"A bit," I say, thinking of that book in the freezer and that picture trying to escape from the page. "That they're best left alone."

She barks a laugh. "Probably, yeah. Ever wondered what it would be like to meet one? Up close and personal?"

"No."

I don't enjoy lying, but every now and then one sort of slips out. It tastes bitter in my mouth. But she doesn't seem to notice and concentrates on stubbing out her fag. She doesn't light another. Her stained fingers twine together in her lap.

"I did. I wasn't much older than you. Had a boyfriend, twenty, and so smooth. Introduced me to this club, he called it. Scared the shit out of me, but I kept going back. Did chanting and that. Candles. Chalk circles on the floor. Once someone had a bottle of blood. Never asked where it came from."

"You were in a cult?" I ask. I try to sound shocked, but I'm not. If anything, I'm impressed, but I don't want her to know that. No kid should ever let their parent know that they've impressed them.

"Sure, I guess. It was all a laugh to them, at the beginning. I was freaked out, but I guess that was part of the game. But then on the night with the blood..."

"The tentacles. You summoned them?"

"Arms," she says, a far-away look in her eyes.

"What?"

"Only the two with hooks are tentacles. The others are arms."

She sounds almost wistful as she gazes out the window, to where the sea waits in the darkness.

"What happened?" I ask, eagerness creeping into my voice, grasping greedily for information.

"He ate Ricky. And Georgina, that bitch. But then it wasn't creepy anymore. It was *real*. I came back the next night, alone, and did the ritual just the same. And I kept coming back every night for years. Until thirteen years ago."

Thirteen years. She had been pregnant with me. Something in me softens towards her as I study her craggy face.

The wet beating is suddenly replaced by a tearing, smashing thud. We both look down the hall. The hollow plywood has hooked spikes poking through in places now. The whole door shudders as the tentacle tries to pull itself free, but it's caught.

"But if you stopped summoning it, why did it start showing up a couple of months ago?" I ask.

Mum turns to me, eyes intense, mouth pinched. "You came of age," she says.

Fear washes over me again, cold and sickening. The tentacles – no, arms – are here for *me*?

"Why?" My voice is very small.

There's a thunderous cracking as the hooks tear themselves free.

Now there's a massive hole in the wood and arms snake their way out. Mum pushes the bedroom door closed without getting up.

"He wants you," she says.

"But *why?*" I ask again, voice now shrill. My hands are trembling, and I push them inside the sleeves of my school jumper.

"Because you're his."

There's nothing I can say to that. I realise my mouth's hanging open but don't bother to shut it. The silence is broken by a thud on the other side of the partition wall. That thing is poking around in my room.

"No," I say at last.

"Don't blame you. Wouldn't believe it myself if I hadn't been there. But trust me, kid, you're his as much as mine." She laughs, one sharp squawk. "Hey, you've been wanting answers. This is why I never gave you any."

I'd feel sick if I had that kind of connection to my body, but I seem to be drifting away. Everything feels so small and insignificant all of a sudden.

"Hey, Marina! Stay with me, girl!" Mum shakes me, and I snap back into the room. "Don't you go drifting off like that. No telling where you might wind up. Or when."

The answers fray at the ends into a thousand smaller questions. Where do I even start? I rub my eyes with my palms but that doesn't help.

"*Why?*" I ask for a third time. "Mum, I don't understand, what are you telling me? That I'm *half monster?* What does it *want*

with me? Why didn't you *say* anything? How did...it...happen?"
Ah, I'm back again. I almost retch at that last thought.

The thumping around in my room has stopped and started up
again on the other side, in the bathroom. There's a splash as one
arm investigates the toilet and a ripping as the shower curtain
gets tangled with another. Mum sighs and reaches for her can.
She takes a swig.

"You know..." She gesticulates with her hands.

"Mum!" I shriek, blood throbbing in my cheeks.

Mum laughs her extra dirty laugh, deep in her throat. But then
she smiles, and her eyes drift out to sea again.

"He wasn't always like this. When we first met he made me
feel...special. Like I was the only person in the universe. And
he was powerful, more powerful than anyone I'd ever known. I
got swept up in the whole thing. And no, he was never caring or
gentle." She brushes the scar on her face. "But I knew I meant
something to him. I was devoted to that bastard and he favoured
me. That was enough. Before you.

"I knew you'd change that. He wouldn't need me anymore and if
he took you, you'd have nobody to look after you. God knows *he*
wouldn't. So I ran. Ran inland.

"D'you remember that little bungalow by the lake? No, you'd
only've been three when we moved away. Lived in a block of flats
overlooking a river. And then that mouldy old shack surrounded
by marshland, you must remember that one."

I did. Mum making me paper boats to float on the river.
Collecting frogspawn from that bog. And Mum growing more
and more insular, surrounding herself with smoke and booze.

And so much water. No matter how hard she'd tried to tear herself away, she'd never quite managed.

"And then we came here when you were ten. Nice school, steady job. Figured he'd given up on you, but that just goes to show how stupid your mum is, hey. And now he's back. For you."

Bitterness. How can she be bitter that the monster's after me, not her? The bubble of anger inflating in my chest starts to push up my throat. The bathroom's gone silent. There's a slippery sound creeping up the bedroom door, and the light coming in the cracks at the edges is blocked out in places. Mum reaches for the baseball bat, propped up against the edge of the bed, and downs the rest of the lager.

"Right. Let's sort this out, once and for all."

The bubble pops before I have a chance to unleash it on her.

"What?" I ask, but she's reaching for the door knob. I scream "No!" at her, but she's already opening it.

It's not just tentacles anymore, or arms even. The hallway is crammed full of squishy grey-green blubber and pale suckers. And right in the middle is a single massive eye, as tall as I am.

"Alright, Your Majesty?" Mum says, swinging the bat. "Long time no see. You're looking well."

There's a sucking, squelching, gurgling sound.

"No thanks to you, love," she replies.

The monster says something again. If I concentrate, I can almost understand. The meaning goes straight into my brain without the need for electrical signals or interpretation. But I'm not thinking about it. My brain has more or less switched off as I stare into that eye.

"No. You can't have her," Mum says. She glances at me over her shoulder, then pokes me with a red fingernail. "Hey. Stay with us, kid."

A slippery arm winds across the carpet and rises, coming at me. I can't remember how to move my legs all of a sudden. Mum smacks it hard with the bat, and it recoils sharply.

"I said 'no,'" she says in a voice I know too well.

"Mum," I croak. "What're you doing? You can't take on an Elder God with a baseball bat."

It's toying with her. I know it is. And her bravado is a lie she tells the world to protect her ego. An armour that is going to drag her down and get her killed.

"Sure I can. See?" And she clouts another arm as it crawls through the doorway.

"But we can't stand against that!"

"I can for a while. And you can climb down the fire escape."

And the terror I felt a second ago shrinks away as anger rushes over me again. But now I'm angry with everything. With Mum, for all the lies. With the monster for existing. With Mum for deciding to sacrifice herself and the monster for letting her think it'll work. And with myself for just standing there...The rage rises up inside my mouth, over my tongue, past my teeth. I open my lips and out it comes.

"No," I say. My voice sounds different; feels different. As though it's vibrating the airwaves in more than one dimension. The eye is staring into me and I can feel its curiosity; its anticipation. Mum stands frozen, like time's stopped. And I know, in that instant, that her entire story was true, is true, will be true. I *am* a child of the Elder God.

"Move," I command my mother, and she levitates a couple of inches, mouth open in an "O" of surprise, and slides through the air further into the bedroom. I step forwards. I realise, in a detached kind of way, that I'm not even angry anymore. I simply *am*.

"You're not needed here. Or wanted," I tell the god.

You are needed, child. And wanted, he tells my brain.

I want it to be true. I imagine myself living as a goddess, having and doing and being whatever I want. That vast, unblinking eye bores into me. The taste of power is tempting. But then I think of Mum and what exposure to that power did to her and the hunger in me dies. That's not who I am. I can see who I am clearly for the first time: powerful, apparently, but not defined by it.

"No. You've had thirteen years to find me. You don't want me. You only want to control me."

I can taste the truth of the words, sweeter than syrup. I *know*, as no mortal can know, what the future could hold. The strands of it stretch out into millions upon millions of minutely different possibilities. In some, I go with him, either peacefully or struggling or unconscious. And in some I stay, either resentful or powerful or unchanged. But there is one. A bright nugget of potential glistening in the estuary of time. This is the future I want. I reach for it.

You can have everything, the voice in my mind promises.

Everything your mother could never give you. You will be a queen, ruling the universes at my side, my beloved daughter...

"I said 'no,'" I say, my voice cool and flat. "I have all that already. My mother loves me and gives me everything I could ever need. I never needed or wanted a father. You will leave us alone."

And there it is. My humanity manifesting alongside my divinity, something he could never do. A lie, from the mouth of a god.

The eye presses forward on a rippling mat of limbs. The hooked tentacles rise and advance. I can feel him doing something to the universe around me. He's changing the world into one where I don't struggle with him, where no attachment to Mum has a hold on me. One of those channels in the river of time that feed into an ocean of darkness.

But I know something that he doesn't. He's trying to switch me off a path where I feel affection for Mum, not knowing that his starting point is wrong. I smirk at him and look for that future I want again. The monster has no clue how to deal with untruth, like oil separating from water. But my life is nothing if not an agitation, and I'm an emulsion of god and mortal. I find that twinkle of promise and carve the fiction of a happy life into the darkness. Then I force myself and Mum and the monster and the universe around us along the roughly-hewn channel of narrative.

There's a loud "pop" in my ears, as though I'm coming up from underwater. I stumble forward a step, disoriented. The universe rearranges itself. The wallpaper stops peeling and brightens as the smoke stains are erased from existence. There is a rushing of air, as the stink of cigarettes and booze is flushed out to make way for the scent of home-cooked meals and fabric softener. I am in a time and a place that hadn't existed before I imagined it and called it into being. A world where my father never bothered to come back and Mum never wanted him to.

And he withdraws, like he's pulled into a vacuum, sucked out through the smashed kitchen window in a flurry of flailing appendages. Into a reality where we weren't worth the effort of pursuing. Mum and I go over to look and every pane of glass has smashed. But there's no sign of him outside.

"We won't be seeing him again," I say, and it's true. I can feel it coiling out from me, snagging on the past and the future and taking hold. The next time I look out the window, the glass is in the frame and the shards are gone from the floor and sink.

Mum looks amazing. Healthy and young. And she smiles at me. It's almost as unsettling as finding an Elder God in your hallway. But her brow is crinkled, trying to remember something.

"What's the matter, Mum?" I ask.

"I...I'm not sure." Her voice is soft and gentle. I barely recognise it. This will take us both some getting used to.

But the human brain is a wonderful thing. She smiles again, as though choosing to forget, a brightness in her eyes.

"Fancy a movie?" she asks. "You can pick."

"Sure," I say, a twang of uncertainty in my voice. Then I decide to embrace this reality. I did create it, after all. "And some ice cream?"

It's about 10.30 by now, but she'll say yes. And there's cookie dough ice cream in the freezer. I know there is, although there wasn't a minute ago.

"Yes please," she says.

She heads to the bedroom to set up the DVD player and I go to the freezer and take out the tub of ice cream. I also remove the frosty book lurking behind a lasagna. When I look at the title now, it reads *The Elder Gods, their history, nature, and control thereof.* I grin at the thought of a mortal attempting to control a god, but I click my fingers and the book winks out of existence, just in case.

With two spoons in one hand and our late-night treat in the other, I go find my mum. I take a peek into my bedroom on my way past. It's clean and tidy, with a plain purple duvet set on the bed and my faultless chemistry homework completed on the desk. An alien sensation flutters in my chest. Contentment. And pride, like I solved an extra tricky equation. For the first time in my life, everything feels balanced and complete. I've been carrying the solutions around inside myself all these years without even realising. I won't ever let uncertainty overwhelm my self-confidence again, I *know* it.

Blood Feathers

Christi Krug

Christi Krug's poetry and fiction have appeared in everything from religious magazines to self-help books to comic book anthologies. She is a Pushcart Prize nominee, and recently served as writer-in-residence at North Cascades Institute. She is a multi-faceted coach of creativity and mindfulness, and the author of Burn Wild: A Writer's Guide to Creative Breakthrough. www.christikrug.com

She ran barefoot through the doors, past the shops, past bicycles and cars. Marshall, Quimby, Raleigh, then 26th, peeling off her leggings as she went, her bare legs pumping along the dusky green school field, beside the happy families, the lithe dogs, the wary picnickers beneath ominous rolling clouds. Now she was nearly naked and the flecks in the night sky were sparks flying up from a campfire burning holes in the world, and she was losing her soul, and yes, it was about time.

It was Friday morning, and the dominant feeling was that of being pinched as she pulled on her leggings. The catch at her tailbone made Ren wonder if her chakras were off. She patted her butt pockets to be sure a bunched-up dryer sheet hadn't hitched a ride. She ran fingertips inside her waistband. Still, the odd crinkle. Hadn't her yoga teacher said the first chakra—or was it the second—was the center of money, sex, and...? She swished dental rinse, spat the blue-green mouthful into the sink. She stared into the mirror, trying to remember the third thing about the second chakra.

Brush in hand, she flung open her daughter's door. Bailey was burrowing under covers, dark hair with the streak of red ribboning over cotton jersey. What, pray tell, was the point of Bailey setting her phone alarm? It shook and buzzed at the edge of the mattress. Her last phone had been run over by a four-wheeler, the disaster of the summer. Without being able to text, Bailey had been separated from her flock.

Something Ren didn't have to worry about. She didn't have friends. She was always about to start a friendship, but then she would back off when the friend was too...something. Louisa, a fellow soprano in choir, so chatty and funny, wore peridot and read comic books. She just kept getting weirder. Ren couldn't have that. She was trying to be solid now, she was obviously a linear person. Doing one thing at a time, herding the kids where they needed to go. She'd quit choir. She had a tiny little reed of a voice, a squeak. Who could compete with Aunt Marva , the former opera singer? Ren was fully occupied being a support, a failsafe, for her family.

She touched the thin wing of Bailey's shoulder blade. "Rise and shine, superstar." She drew circles on Bailey's back. With her other hand she brushed her own hair. It was wild today.

Bailey grabbed her pillow and planted it over the back of her head, sealed by her forearms.

"Now." Ren yanked the pillow to the floor. Her anger spurted then thinned to a dripping faucet. She sighed. "You can't be late again. It's only the third week of school."

Her problem was Bailey. Or maybe her own ineptness. Her brain issue made her a horrible teacher of life skills.

Her problem was *not* being late for work. Fridays at the nonprofit were so chill that Ella brought her grandkid and Brittany made a run to Voodoo Doughnuts. Work was a break from the care, feeding, and transport of the humans she lived with. And from their need to be entertained.

It was Charlie who needed to be entertained. Once Bailey was off with friends, and Jackson was with his mom, well, then Charlie expected Ren to "spend time with him," to be his wife, playmate, and helper, running errands all Saturday, and on Sunday kayaking, then going to dinner, then seeing a movie, and afterward, turning on the sizzle, whether she felt sizzle or not. Lately, not.

Her problem was Charlie.

Tonight was Aunt Marva's birthday dinner.

Her problem was she couldn't keep this up anymore.

When Bailey's feet touched floor, Ren ran into the kitchen and threw together almond butter and jelly. She knew Bailey would supplement with preserved poisons from the vending machine. She tucked the lunch inside her daughter's backpack. Her knuckles hit metal. "What the—?"

Ren pulled out a sepia photograph in a tinny frame. Dark eyes stared from a pale face. A feather headband swept the high forehead. "Cornelia," she breathed.

Bailey thundered down the stairs. "Where did you get this?" asked Ren. "Theater project," Bailey said, snatching socks from a laundry basket. "We're supposed to create a show about a distinctive member of our family."

"But you never knew Cousin Cornelia," Ren said, after they got in the car.

"I visited her that one time, remember?"

Ren squared her shoulders, squinting at a traffic light. Her left elbow itched. "Maybe," she said. Anything before the accident was hazy.

"She lived in Washington," said Bailey, holding her mascara wand aloft. She adjusted the passenger mirror. "Near the Snowhome River."

Ren paused. "Snohomish?"

Bailey waved her mascara. "Whatever. I was little and stayed a weekend. It was at the start of the school year. She told me stories. Also, we went to this old school, Wagner something, and watched all these birds do a migration thing. Thousands and thousands swirling all around the roof."

Ren dodged Bailey's mascara. She saw in her mind's haze Cornelia's old farmhouse, the massive red brick chimney. "Did she die?" asked Ren. For the life of her, it was one more thing she couldn't remember.

Bailey capped her mascara and picked up her phone. "She disappeared. It was complicated. I hate having to tell you everything."

Ren had lost her family long ago, except for Cornelia, the old cousin twice-or-thrice removed who'd had six children. Ren didn't remember the kids; besides, they'd long ago flown the coop. Ren remembered Cornelia's eyes, small and shiny as flax seeds. It was strange not having a family like other people, but you got used to it. Now that she had Charlie's family, it wasn't all that it was cracked up to be. Aunt Marva, a tyrant, a one-time opera star, a clock-watcher.

But that was okay, Ren was a linear person.

She worked half a day at the nonprofit, then headed home. She flipped on public radio. The Vaux's swifts were "plummeting into the chimney at Chapman School tonight around 8 pm." Other cities had weather reports; Portland had bird reports. She snapped off OPB and ran through her checklist: buy groceries, get gift bag, make calls—car repair shop, plumber. She dashed into the house and wondered if there was time for a dip at the pool. But she'd lost her padlock.

Charles kept every lock, along with every key, keys to locks from houses left long ago, keys and the sewing kits they give in hotels. She rifled through his dresser drawer and found six buttons, half-used sunscreen, and an old pair of binoculars. She pushed the assortment aside until she found a padlock. It was in a plastic box.

There was something else in the box.

A ring of feathers. Intricate, silvery feathers, comprising a tiny, dusky gray band. Or it might have been blue, or black, with a shifting of light.

It was the same feeling she'd had seeing Cornelia's photograph—as if that regal face were trying to tell her something.

Something she didn't remember.

The stupid accident.

This ring, it should be hers, should it not?

She pulled it over her finger, but it didn't fit. Not even on the pinky. She put it in her back pocket. And then felt her tailbone. Still crinkly.

Which made her worry.

Was this a skin lesion? Cancer?

Charles was uptight about money and who knew if insurance would cover this. She pulled off her sweater, tugged down her leggings, and twisted around to the mirror. There it was: a stiff spiny thing, like a long thin tooth, emerging from her tailbone.

She couldn't tell Charles or he'd freak. He'd insist she see *his* dermatologist, just like he insisted she use his plumber, repair shop, and even hairdresser. She disliked his people. Conventional to the core. But she was, too, wasn't she? It was easy to go his way with things, because, after all, what did she know? Her brain could only go as far back as coming home from the hospital after the accident, Charles driving the copper-colored Acura, a couple of months before they got married.

She didn't remember much of Bailey's Dad. She could see herself sneaking into the garage, weeks after their separation, rifling through the beat-up filing cabinet for papers. For identification. For things she'd never recovered. . . she blinked. The feathered ring? But then, she must've found it, before Charles stashed it away. She felt hollow, porous, as she sped across town to Bailey. Couldn't you pick a past the way you opened your car door to a passenger? *You look fine. Come on in and be my own.*

She parked and scanned faces as bodies spilled out of school doors. So many girls wore skimpy things. *In my day we didn't show bra straps*, she thought. We were svelte, aerodynamic.

But she wasn't exactly sure.

Ren rested her chin on the steering wheel. The sun warmed the car leather, raising scents of sweat, sour milk, cat, and trapped french fries.

Her elbow ached. She touched it, and an arrow of pain shivered along her arm to the small bones of her neck. What if she had been someone else before the accident? What if she'd been an artist?

The closest she'd come to creation was yesterday. At the craft store, she bought weather-beaten reminders of a simpler time.

Okay, made in a factory and steeped in chemicals, but still. She'd flung all her distressed wood and twiggy things onto the kitchen table. The hot glue gun smelled like Tupperware melting in the dishwasher, yet was not altogether unpleasant.

Late into the night, she sorted, arranged, and glued. It had felt right, making the gift.

. . . for Aunt Marva's dinner – *tonight!*

Her blood pressure quickened. Charles hated when she was late.

Where are you? she texted Bailey.

She thought of her neighbor, Geneva, getting her PhD. Her kids always on time. Now there was a woman Ren should emulate, especially according to Charlie. But Ren never fit in with other moms, the ones without mixed families, or the women without kids. Ren's rhythms were different. Every change of season pulled at her. September was the worst.

She bolted out of the car, stood by the brick entry. She had an impulse to cling to the wall, to pull herself upward. She reached both hands, pressing fingertips into mortar, holding her body erect, close to the brick, as if preparing to cling tight for a long time.

"Mom!"—Bailey's voice delivered the word with at least two syllables—"I told you, I had to stay after for the Theater project, don't you ever hear me?"

Ren shook herself as her daughter followed her back to the SUV. In the passenger seat, Bailey crossed her arms, miffed. But then she softened. She took off a purple hat draped with an enormous peacock feather, and her deep brown hair with its red streak billowed onto her shoulders. She touched the hat brim with interest.

It sported a row of silver sequins alternating with thin black threads and a gold magnifying glass. Ren opened her mouth in an "O" of curiosity.

"Cousin Cornelia's hat," explained Bailey. "The kind of thing she used to wear. She would go around collecting feathers and looking at them under the magnifying glass. Don't you remember? She called the feathers, 'dream castoffs'. Peacock isn't right, but that's all I could find. And here, with the sequins, these are thistle seeds. Some birds are bug feeders, but remember, she used to feed the birds? She had a hundred birds coming to her feeders every day, I bet."

Ren pulled onto I-5 which was already slowing. Teaching Bailey to drive was going to be brutal. Charles barely let *Ren* behind the wheel. When a situation was unpredictable, he avoided it.

"These pics are so crazy," Bailey said, scrolling through screens on her phone, grinning. "Here I am in our play, holding my arms up in a cloud of steam. It's supposed to be a magic cloud of birds, but we have to use dry ice. That's how Cornelia disappears, where she's last seen."

Ren only caught every other word. "Where did this story come from?"

"It's in the old clipping from the Everett Herald. Now do you remember?"

Left onto Northwest 23rd, just missing a silver Prius.

Hawwnk!

"Watch it, Mom!"

How was a person supposed to see through parked cars?

Aunt Marva's gift tumbled onto the floor from the back seat. All her hard work. *Please don't be broken.*

She limped in her heels ahead of Bailey toward Papa Haydn's. As she went, she pulled up her gray sleeve. A slim spur of bone jutted from her elbow. Something dark, like a blood blister, was emerging from the flesh.

She gasped and covered the arm.

Aunt Marva, Jackson, and Charles were in the back corner of the restaurant. Aunt Marva was giving her that look.

Jackson glanced up. He pushed his glasses higher up on his freckled nose and went back to scanning the menu, his long form folded over the table.

"I was worried because you didn't answer your cell," said Charles.

Ren clapped her hand over the crinkly small of her back. Her body, it knew something. "Traffic," she said, as Aunt Marva's eyes flashed out of sync with that artificial smile. Bailey sat, flipped her hair over her shoulder, and picked up the menu.

"Didn't you come straight from school?" asked Charles.

"Five minutes," Ren breathed. "I'm late by FIVE MINUTES, okay!" She swallowed hard, trying to even out her heartbeat.

Everyone looked away. She took the moment to squeeze past Charles into the seat by the window. "Well, there's always traffic now, isn't there?" broke in Aunt Marva. "Arnie used to miss my birthday and every year I'd tell him, 'Some things happen whether you're ready or not, so you might as well get ready.'"

Ren's chest tightened.

"And ready means organized." Aunt Marva laughed musically, and her matte lipsticked lips curled up at the ends, but her eyes were hard. "Something you may have been before your accident. Of course, I didn't know you well, then.

"Organized," she continued. "Is that a dirty word for you, Ren? Do you just *hate* that word?" Aunt Marva laughed again, patted the back of her red curls, then exclaimed over the menu. "Crab cakes. Isn't it funny how much I love crab cakes when I hate crab?"

Marigolds nodded from the centerpiece, making Ren think of clowns. A tiny spider, hanging from a single strand, bobbed toward her water glass. Without thinking, she inched forward into the air, opened her mouth, and enclosed the spider inside. She swallowed.

Her husband gaped at her, eyebrows high in alarm.

Glasses were clinking and the wait staff was singing "Happy Birthday" three tables over. No one but Charles had noticed.

Ren leaned back, closed her eyes. The taste in her mouth was nutty, wonderful.

She thought back to the start of their marriage. Hadn't they met birdwatching? That's what he'd told her, another memory she couldn't resurrect. Charles had since stopped birding. He was in high demand at his architectural firm, and less inclined to go out in the rain.

What she missed was rain, and air, and wind.

Maybe she had come to him some other way. That was all so long ago.

And now her right elbow was throbbing. A movement outside the window caught her eye. A twitch in the maple tree, a sparrow.

"Couldn't we change the plan?" Ren had asked Charles that morning as he got ready for work. "Do something unexpected? I heard the swifts are roosting at Chapman—"

"Huh?" Charles was working his belt through his pants.

"That bird thing. You know. They come every year and roost in the chimney of the ancient school building. It's a nature experience, how they descend all at once. We could walk over after dessert."

"Honey, you know Marva's arthritis makes walking difficult."

"Well, we can drive first. Then we can sit on a blanket."

"Her sciatica makes it impossible to sit. Why can't you be more understanding?" He sighed, fishing for the back loop. "Why do you always make everything so difficult?" He fastened the buckle, stepped over and kissed her quickly.

Now she scanned the sky, seeing dark clouds, trees, buildings. Shapes she had seen in another lifetime.

The accident, it happened here. Northwest Portland. She remembered in a flash. She'd been on her way...to Food Front?... getting provisions.

"Here." She picked up the beribboned bag on the restaurant seat beside her and thrust it at Aunt Marva.

"Oh, you shouldn't have!" Aunt Marva clasped her hands over her chest. She lifted the tissue from the bag. There was an awkward silence as the tissue fell away and she held the contents. "It's...a nest."

"A swag," said Ren, her voice catching in her throat. It did look like a nest, in a squared saucer shape. It hadn't occurred to her until now.

Jackson blinked, a complete poker face. He took an enormous mouthful of Georgian peanut butter mousse. Bailey held her phone up to her mom as if to change the subject. "Did I show you the cast photo?" But Ren had already seen the look of horror that said, *What is wrong with my mother?*

The Bocconi Dulce tilted on Ren's plate, collapsing. It was sweet, too sweet. What she craved was another spider, just the size of a dandelion seed, a wish pushed out from a stem of wishes, a bloomed thing only she could taste. What became of all unclaimed wishes blowing all over the world?

Charles' fork clinked against the plate as he severed corners of the Hood River Apple Crisp. Ren was dumbfounded that there were people who put time and energy into such elaborate dishes. What she set on the dinner table lately were dry, natty, things, like lentils she boiled endlessly. She was taken with chia seeds.

She wanted her foods to be like her—why take up space in the world? She was small, dry and drab. The moisture had been pressed out.

Her dreams were lost things resurfacing. Besides the pinch at her tailbone, she felt a lump directly beneath her. That feathered ring. With one hand she reached behind, brushing her leggings pocket.

"It's getting dark," she whispered, feeling her heartbeat slow, as if she were crouching at the starting line of a race. "They're coming at dusk. I may not get another chance..."

Charles looked away. As if he hadn't heard.

Ren stared out the window at a wisp of cloud. Under the table, she withdrew her hand from her pocket. She spread her white cloth napkin over the sinewy tops of her hands and commanded them to be still.

A fat raindrop fell, then another. Ren squeezed past Charles, sliding out of the booth. "I've got to go...I...the swifts."

Her hands shook as she tossed her white napkin on the table. Her family stared, stunned. She did not grab her purse.

Charles barked, "Sit down!"

She could feel all eyes in the restaurant, curious, amused, hypothesizing. Her daughter was texting furiously, trying to fade into the artwork on the wall. Her ankles wobbled in high heels as she raced forward.

She kicked off her shoes and ran, heart in throat, blood behind her eyes.

She ran barefoot through the doors, past the shops, past bicycles and cars. She jogged left onto Marshall, hung another left at Quimby, then at Raleigh, zigzagging to 26th, peeling off her leggings as she went, her bare legs pumping along the dusky green school field, and she shed the rest of her clothes as she ran, reaching the happy families, the lithe dogs, the wary picnickers beneath ominous rolling clouds. The flecks in the night sky were sparks flying up from a campfire burning holes in the world, and she was losing her soul, and yes, she was finding it again, and yes, it was about time.

They were crying, shouting directions, making promises, declaring truces, making threats. This one was terrified by the hawk watching from the fir tree. That one chattered about running behind schedule. Another held forth about wind currents, and there were so many words for winds, and oh my God, she could hear all their words and feel their histories, knowing that among them were the shapeshifting ones, like Cornelia had been, living for a time as humans and then returning to their own. She felt the bones behind her elbows, each growing feathers, dark and filled with blood, and her tailbone balancing her center, elongating, sprouting, and her feet so light, no longer a part of any body she'd known.

And she remembered what was in her pocket, and she placed the silky feather-webbed ring onto her hooked claw, not talon, swifts didn't have talons, and it slipped into place easily, and she smiled over all the human beings converging to watch her people, all the landlocked humans as they wandered and trailed and pecked like chickens. They had no wings.

And one man was standing on the curb next to a red-haired old woman and two young, thin ones who were standing and looking.

And the rain stopped, but these four humans had rain on their faces. They turned their faces to the sky.

"She remembers her old life now, and she has to go back!" cried the one with the long, dark feathers and streak of red. "Just like Cornelia!"

Her heart called to them, her heart so much smaller, yet so much lighter, so bright, beating fast and slow at the same time. She could not stop. Her mind that had learned to remember, had also learned to forget. And as the wind took her, and she unfurled her new wings, she found a word: "Power. The second chakra is the center of power." Her last human thought.

The Blinded God

Greta Hayer

Greta Hayer is a writer living in New Orleans. Her fiction has appeared in Beneath Ceaseless Skies and nonfiction in Booth and Flint Hills Review. She received a bachelor's degree in history from the College of Wooster, where she studied fairy tales and medieval medicine.

My Eyes stands at the edge of the cliff, and I try to remember the way the sky looks behind him.

"Can you really not see any of this, Thea?" he asks me.

"High Priestess Thea," I correct him gently, since he's new to the temple and still learning our ways. I can feel the setting sun, warm on my face, and feel the wind rushing past, carrying a hint of night in its gusts, but my eyes see only shadows of the sun, a murky gold against black. I can sense the blindfold, more for the neophyte's sake than my own, resting over my eyes, the thin weave of my dress, the way the grass brushes against my bare feet. And I remember the cliff vividly, the way the sharp rocks break up the sea, the way the foaming waves mimic the wisps of clouds. The sky was a myriad of colors when last I saw it, rose and gold and red. I remember the light reflecting on the water and the verdant green of the pastures.

But I only have memories, for I am blind.

"It's beautiful," the neophyte says. "Would you like me to describe it to you?"

I laugh, though I shouldn't be laughing. I am one of the High Priestesses of the Blinded God, and I have a certain aloofness and sagacity I am, by duty, supposed to embody. But I cannot help myself. I couldn't forget these cliffs if I wanted to. It is where I performed my blinding ceremony years ago. It is the last image imprinted on my memory before I watched the dark point of the knife draw close.

I tell the neophyte that I'm not laughing at him. He is, after all, my Eyes. This is his duty, until, gods willing, he becomes a proper priest, maybe even a blind one. I reach out my hand. "Let us return to the temple."

The neophyte's hand is soft, uncalloused. He did not come from a hard life, that much is clear from his accent and manners, and his hand tells the story of a boy who never gripped sword, or spear, or hoe. Once dedicated to the temple, we are supposed to leave our old lives behind us, but sometimes those lives linger in our bodies. A hand like his couldn't lie, couldn't pretend he was warrior, or shepherd, or slave. I wonder, not for the first time since he became my Eyes a few days ago, why he joined the temple. The Blinded God, the god of fate and future, is certainly not the most generous or undemanding of the pantheon; there are plenty of soft gods who don't require their devotees to stick hot knives in their eyes. Does he really have faith enough to make the sacrifice the temple will one day demand of him?

The walk back to the temple is a short one, and my Eyes guides me by hand. I don't need his help. I've taken this journey hundreds of times. I know every rock, every bend in the path. Soon, I am stepping nimbly up the marble steps to the temple, cold and smooth under my feet. I can hear the fountain, the voices of other priests, and priestesses, and their assorted attendants. I can identify individual voices, echoing around the marble. I know everyone here.

"Thea of the True Sight," the seneschal, keeper of the temple, calls my name and formal epithet, and I tense in anticipation. I don't know what he will say, but he sounds solemn and ceremonial. "Come, speak with me."

I follow his voice, my neophyte trailing behind me with shuffling sandals. The seneschal, the official caretaker of the temple and only high ranking cleric allowed to keep his sight, directs me to sit near one of the fountains, most likely so the sound or running water will mask our words. It is a strange thing, privacy in a temple of the blind. Secrets are whispered but still overheard. The ears of the blind are sharp. And yet our sighted servants know so many things about us that we don't know ourselves. Is the seneschal still straight-backed and red-haired? Or has he stooped in his age and turned grey?

"Thea, I have a task for you," the seneschal says quietly. I sense my Eyes standing behind me, but there are no other footsteps, no other breaths.

"Anything," I say because I am a high priestess, not a god. Even we have duties we must attend to.

"The Blinded God's amphora must be brought from the city of Aquilla to the temple. I have received information that people are..." I hear him drum his fingers against the bench. "Well, desecrating is one word for it. I would not deem to soil your ears with more description."

I want to object, fear coursing through me. The outside world is chaos and disorder, but a high priestess should not be afraid. I swallow it, and the fear churns in my stomach like too much wine.

I turn to the seneschal, and a vision of True Sight flashes before me. I see him, older than I remember, just as grey as I imagined. His nose is longer, with pores like craters. He's looking over my shoulder at my Eyes, and I want to turn my head, but the vision is just of the senechal, the deep furrows in his forehead. He is worried.

"You will have your Eyes as a guide," he continues.

I can still see the seneschal with the True Sight. I see his chapped lips and his nose hairs. I see a pimple on his chin. "But when I sent a lower order priest, they refused him. They will not refuse a priestess with the True Sight."

There are five other high priestesses with the True Sight, five others that could have been picked. I try to feel honored by the responsibility, just as I try to feel honored by the Sight, but I cannot help the creep of dread. I don't want to leave the safety of the Temple, the only home I've ever had.

I blink, and the vision of the seneschal leaves me. I am alone in my world of shadows again. I feel disoriented. I want to sit down.

I nod, knowing the seneschal can see.

***

We are on the road by dawn. I feel the darkness, damp and chill on my lips. I have never before ridden, and it is hard to trust, but the mare's steady, swaying footsteps lull my nervous heart, and my Eyes murmurs to her occasionally in a calm, comforting voice, which helps me as well. I am not comfortable around horses. They are so large, and I am never quite certain where their feet are placed. I wish for a flash of the True Sight, but, instead, my body shifts from side to side, moving forward into the darkness.

I try to think of what my vision means. Though I am gifted with the True Sight, visions do not occur frequently. It often comes in moments of importance or danger. I try to interpret symbols from the image of the seneschal, but there is no god of old men, and no meaning I can make out from the crevices of his face.

"What is your name?" I ask my Eyes. I am embarrassed that I don't know.

"Timon, priestess."

He leads the mare for a long time under a sweltering noon sun before he speaks again. "What did you do before you entered the temple?" Timon asks.

"We leave our lives when we swear ourselves to the Blinded God," I remind him, the words that are drilled into every neophyte's head when they first arrive.

"All right." I hear him sigh. "It's just such a long walk."

I say nothing, but I am growing bored as well. I assumed that a holy mission for the Blinded God Himself would give me strength, but it is difficult to look forward to days of silent plodding. My back hurts, and my blindfold is soaked in sweat. Timon's steps sound weary, a fraction slower than they were that morning.

"You may tell me about yourself," I offer.

"Oh." He sounds shocked, maybe a little disappointed. I know there are rumors about me; I've heard them echoing through the temple, reverberating in the marble halls. When I blinded myself on the cliffs, I was not only the youngest priestess to do so, but also the youngest to gain the True Sight. People speak of me with awe, a reverence I don't deserve. I can't speak of my life before to Timon because, for me, there is no life before. My first memories are of the temple, of the blind priests and priestesses describing how to tend a garden or speak the psalms. I was left at the temple door swaddled in soft linen. That was my life before.

"My father has seven sons," Timon says. "I am the seventh."

"The lucky," I say. There are seven gods in our pantheon. The seventh, the last-born child of Time and Earth, is Luck himself.

"The unwanted," Timon mutters, quiet enough that any other person might not have heard him.

"Why do you say that?"

"My father has sons for everything. An heir, a soldier, a scholar, a banker, another soldier, even a poet. I didn't want to do what my father wanted me to do."

"And what was that?"

"He said he needed a son who knew the will of the gods. He had everything arranged with the temple of The Brightest God. I'd have every luxury I could ask for. I wouldn't even have to make a vow of chastity." He laughs harshly. "Anyway, when he told me that, explained that he had my life so perfectly ordered, I walked out of his villa and went straight to the local temple of the Blinded God."

"Life in our temple is ordered." I can't help the trace of defensiveness in my voice. "Do you regret your choice?" I think about asking him if he regrets his vow of chastity as well, but my stomach twinges nervously at my own audacity. I feel very hot.

"I wanted to make my own choice," Timon says. "I wanted to do something important that no one can take back."

This, I realize, is a thought he has had many times, but has never spoken aloud. I don't press him, but the sentiment sits heavy inside of me, like I am now carrying his burden too.

I wish I could see his face.

We travel another few hours before he interrupts my meditations. "Why does the seneschal want the amphora?"

"The amphora is special to the Blinded God." I know the scripture better than I know anything, and I ramble off the story easily, stealing my teacher's words. "Before, when he was the Sighted One, when he walked the land like mortals, he Saw all that was and all that would be. He fell in love with a human woman."

"I know that story," Timon says. "She was a slave girl, picking berries along the road, right, Priestess?"

"Yes. And he saw her future and her past. He knew she would be beaten by her master for dallying to gather the berries when she was supposed to be bringing his goats to be milked. He knew she would suffer an infection from those wounds. He knew that he could do nothing to save her or stop this fate, and, though he never spoke a word to her, so consumed was he with love that he knew he would suffer for eternity, watching her fate unravel while he was helpless."

"So he went to the cliffs."

"Yes," I said. He has been paying attention in his studies. "The very cliffs where our temple now stands. He looked out at the sunset and drove knives through his eyes. Then he poured wine into the wounds to purify them. Wine, you see, from the very amphora we are sent to collect."

"Oh." His feet shuffle forward a few more steps. "Did you pour wine over your eyes..." He hesitates. "After?"

"Yes." I say, thinking back to the sting. They said it was to clean the wound, but I remember the priestess who blinded herself before me, drenched in red wine, and how it stained her white robe. It had seemed like she was covered in blood. "But, like the Blinded God, I continued to see after the blinding. His ceremony did nothing to stop his pain. The slave girl still died, and the Blinded God now watches it happen, over and over again, in his eternal agony."

"Do you think that using the amphora will give more priests the True Sight?" Timon asks.

It hasn't occurred to me, though I instantly wonder if that is the seneschal's real motivation behind my quest. The True Sight seems so arbitrary, and when I once voiced that opinion when I was a neophyte, a priestess slapped me across the cheek. I don't know why I have been chosen to receive the gift over any of the other devotees; I am not holier or wiser or better than the others. I doubt the Sight has anything to do with the pot from which the cleansing wine came. But I keep that thought to myself, since it is not a particularly faithful one. If I was a better priestess, I would follow the seneschal's orders without question, for the good of the temple.

"Perhaps," I say, trying to seem properly devout. "The Blinded God works mysteriously."

We arrive at the inn when the sun is setting, the bright light directly on my face. Timon takes care of the horse while I wait outside, listening. It is a small village, and I can tell much about it from the sound and smells. Manure, a cooking fire, the scents of piss and wine. I hear the innkeep arguing with someone, complaining of a hole someone dug behind his property. I hear chatter and gossip, but the voices quiet as they near me, either reverent or in fear. No one speaks to me, and I wonder if I am frightening to look upon. The blindfold covers my eyes so that no one sees my cloudy pupils, something that used to frighten me when I was a child looking into the faces of the older priests and priestesses. I am dressed simply, with no weapon or means of intimidation. Still, people walk by me without even a word of hello.

I wonder, not for the first time, what I look like. Am I really so hideous that no one dares speak to me? There are no mirrors in the temple, and I blinded myself when I was just a girl, so I have few hints to my own appearance now, ten years after. I know some priestesses have their Eyes describe to them their faces, and when they hear of their wrinkles, dripping down their cheeks like wax, they weep. I am too afraid to ask.

I hope Timon finds me beautiful.

I catch myself at the thought. That kind of thinking comes dangerously close to launching into an unchaste fantasy. I am a high priestess, I remind myself. If I am blushing when he returns to help me to my room, I cannot know. He takes my hand and leads me to the bedchamber, and after he leaves, I cradle my hand to my cheek where I imagine I feel the warmth from his skin.

I feel the room grow cooler, and night settles. I feel very lonely. I mumble prayers to the Blinded God in the room while mice squeak between the thin walls. I hear raised voices and men drinking, and I stumble to my door to make sure it is locked. My Eyes sleeps in the stable with the horse, so far away. I stub my toe as I climb back into bed, and I pull the blanket taut around me, though the evening is hot. I have never been so far away from home.

***

We arrive in the city, and it smells even worse than I imagined. The heavy press of bodies, the reek of animals, the odor of curing leather. I feel sick as we make our way through the streets. I can't see the people, but I hear them, shoving and shouting and calling out the price of fish. I hear babies crying and mothers trying to shush them. I sit rigid on the horse. "Please don't let them touch me," I whisper to Timon, and I'm not sure if he hears. I feel the press of sound and heat coming at me from all directions. I hope for a moment of True Sight, to help me navigate, but I am stuck in blindness, each plod of hooves taking me deeper into the chaos.

My hands are tight on the pommel of the saddle. I feel my heart pounding. I hear everything, the voices cascading over each other like a waterfall. I am drowning in sound, in smells and shouts. The city presses on me. I move my lips to a familiar prayer, but it brings me no comfort. I want to cry out to Timon for help, but I don't know what he could do.

Eventually, the voices fade into the distance, and the clip of the horse's hooves changes tenor, from the sharpness of stone to the clear ring of marble. Timon stops the mare. "We're in the temple, Priestess Thea. It's okay now."

I nearly collapse when he helps me dismount. I feel shaken from the noise of the city, overwhelmed in every sense I have left. Timon guides me to a reflecting pool, and I listen to the water splash against stone. A poor substitute for the cleansing crash of waves and wind at the coast.

I try to imagine the temple's beauty, but I can't. I can still smell the city beyond, its leather, and metal, and bread, and blood. The scent of urine never disappears here, and even now, as summer begins its fade, the city still sweats profusely.

The Blinded God's temple in the city is much smaller than the one I grew up in, and I hear snippets of whispers from the other priests and priestesses, but they give me a wide berth. Some are blind, but none are True Sighted. When Timon leads me through the temple, he tells me of the deepness of their bows, the grandness of the chamber they provide for me, but I can hear the fear in their voices.

"They seem so afraid," I say to Timon when we're alone in my chamber. "Like they dare not speak to me, but only to you."

"They might not have seen someone with the True Sight before," Timon says. "I hadn't until I met you."

I nod, but I still worry. Something feels off-kilter. "Perhaps the owners of the amphora are not eager to give it up." I try to sound relaxed, but I know something is going to happen on this mission. I had the vision when the seneschal told me the plan, and even within temple walls, I don't feel safe.

Before he leaves me, Timon clears his throat. "Priestess Thea, I just wanted to say..." He hesitates. "I didn't have much faith before this trip. You know my story. But this journey, with you. I see your devotion, and I envy it. I am glad I joined the Blinded God's temple. I am glad you taught me what it means to believe."

"Thank you," I say numbly. I do not think I was a great example of devotion, but I resolve to be better. To be an example Timon can respect.

He closes my door behind him.

***

We are taken to see the amphora by an anxious priest who speaks very quickly and walks just as fast. He's still sighted and has postponed his blinding ceremony until the amphora can be returned to the temple.

"Prince Claudio, well, you must know all about the prince," the priest says, as Timon guides me through the streets. They're quieter today than when we first came to the city, but I still feel disoriented and confused by the mix of noise and voices.

"I know almost nothing about the prince," I say. "We of the Blinded God are not supposed to follow politics."

"Oh, yes. Yes. I suppose that must be. In the capital, it's hard to keep from politics." He giggles nervously, and it sounds like a woman's laugh. "It is good we do, or else we never would have known the amphora was being used so...immodestly."

The prince is in a private bathhouse, and as soon as we enter, I feel clouded by steam and heat and the smell of bodies. I try to take a deep breath, but the wet air sticks in my lungs. My heart begins to race. The floor beneath my feet, tile by the sound of it, is slippery.

Timon puts a hand on my forearm. "Twenty steps until we pass through this room, Thea."

I nod, and my tension releases somewhat. He speaks to me in the same gentle tone he used to talk to the mare, but instead of taking offense, I lean into him as he leads me out of the room.

We move through a creaking door, and then I feel the sun in my face. I hear water splashing and bouncing off stone. I hear laughter and shouts of joy, as well as crude moans of pleasure. I face forward, resolute.

And then the True Sight flashes, and I see the amphora.

It is an ordinary jug of ordinary proportions. The sides are carved with detailed pictures, but the craftsmanship is no more noteworthy than the amphoras used at the temple. I fail to see the importance of the object or why people care so much for it. There is nothing divine that is recognizable, besides the story carved on its side.

I feel deflated. All this way for a simple jug. I take a deep breath and force myself to trust the faith that brought me here, and, long ago, to the cliffs over the roaring ocean, a hot knife in my hand. I feel the pressure of Timon's confession. I want to show him the true meaning of faith.

Surely, the seneschal could see something in the amphora that I cannot. And yet, the Blinded God granted me the True Sight. If the amphora is so undoubtedly important, shouldn't I be able to see it?

Before the True Sight fades, I take in the man holding the amphora. He sits in the water of the large pool and drinks directly from the sacred amphora's rim, rude but not sacrilegious. He's rather young, perhaps midway between twenty and thirty, and he's very handsome. He pulls the amphora from his lips, which are purpled now from wine, and he laughs and splashes the naked woman by his side. She kisses him and slips her hand down his chest and under the water.

There are many girls, most naked, and a few other men who wear the robes of the senate. Everyone seems to be laughing at a joke I don't understand.

My sight begins to flicker, and I see visions that are so quick I only see parts of faces, mouths open too large, eyes squinting against the light. My vision keeps flashing, and I hold my hands over my eyes, but True Sight doesn't work like that. I see grey hair on a man's chest and a big hand pressing tight fingers to a slim waist. I see a firm breast with a brown nipple, a smile that has nothing to do with joy or mirth but something cruel. I see the purple teeth of a man who has drunk too much wine. All around me, the sound of the bathers swells.

"Priestess, I'm here," Timon says softly.

Suddenly, the bathhouse breaks into still calm. My vision returns to blessed darkness. Timon squeezes my arm, and the Sight fades.

Somehow, the bathhouse is less disturbing in the darkness.

"I am Thea, High Priestess of the Blinded God Himself. I have been sent to retrieve his sacred amphora." I point to the prince and his whore.

The prince laughs. "This?"

I assume he holds up the amphora. I hear liquid sloshing in a ceramic. "It is a sacred vessel," I say.

"How dare you demand the prince's amphora? He is heir to the entire empire," a male voice shouts from the other side of the bathhouse, and everyone starts expressing their opinions at once. Silky female voices purr about Claudio's power; gruff male ones renounce me and my mission, even my god. People seem to hate the idea that I would come into the prince's life and demand something from him. They themselves seem to have had to pry every taste of generosity from him with coy glances and pouches of gold coins.

I stand very still, trying to hear every word.

And then a name slips out between the protests. *Timon.*

"Timon of Boros?" The prince repeats, and the rest of the voices simmer away. "That's you, Timon? I almost didn't recognize you. You look so much, well, holier, than last time we spoke."

Timon's grip on my arm tightens. "We leave our lives when we swear ourselves to the Blinded God."

The prince laughs. "Come now, you're not really going to blind yourself just to rebel against your father, are you, Timon?"

I feel Timon's arm shake. With anger? Fear? Is he holding back tears? I speak up. "We have come for the amphora."

The prince sighs heavily. "Fine. What need do I have of this? I have a hundred amphoras. No, a thousand. This one means nothing to me."

"May the Blinded God bless you with a good fate," I say, a traditional benediction, but my heart isn't in the words.

"It's not for the Blinded God that I do this," the prince corrects me, and he doesn't need to finish his thought for me to understand.

I am not the messenger sent to pick up the vessel; it is Timon. The seneschal must know of their relationship, and used Timon's former life to influence the outcome of this moment. I feel used, dirty almost. I had thought the temple was above such things.

Timon narrates the next events to me. Though there are protests, the prince, fully naked, rises from the water and hands the amphora to a gold-collared slave, who returns a few moments later with the vessel cleaned. I open my hands and receive it, and still, I feel no click of rightness or any semblance of power from the pottery. The temple had broken its own rules for a simple jug. I try not to look disappointed.

People continue to complain, even as we wish the prince well and take our leave of the bathhouse. In the room of steam and sweat, I hear a whisper, a man's voice I can't recognize, "You'll regret this."

I'm not sure if the threat is meant for Timon or me.

***

Besides the ominous threat, obtaining the amphora is much easier than I expected. I berate myself for the way I let my anxieties overtake me. I put the strange threat into the back of my head, push aside my worry about being in the city and an unknown temple, and I relax. Tomorrow, we will go home.

Timon bids me good night and leaves me at the door of my room. His chambers are with the rest of the Eyes, a long stretch of marble hallway away. I wish he could sleep at the foot of my bed as some Eyes do at our temple, and I feel a thrill of anticipation that, when we are on the road, we might share a room. A high priestess, especially one blessed with the True Sight, should not have those fantasies, but I cannot help myself.

The amphora sits, wrapped in a soft cloth, with the rest of my belongings.

I lie in bed, fantasizing about the return journey and recalling my vow of chastity. Before long, I am asleep.

I wake in the night, the bugs chirping outside the window. "Timon?" I call, but there is no answer, just insects singing in the hot night. I smell something acrid, and I cough. Smoke. Something is on fire. I realize it's not bugs outside the window but the crack and roar of flames. I stumble out of bed to the door, but the handle is hot and burns my palm. Is the fire in the room? I can't tell. I'm sweating, and my hand hurts.

I cross the room, back to where the window stands. I test with the back of my hand this time; the glass is hot. I'm trapped, and I feel fear like I have never experienced before, even when I brought the knife to my eyes. "Ah," I cry, not sure how to make the words I need, or what words I need in the first place. "Ahh." I repeat again, stupidly, helplessly.

The Sight comes to me like it did in the bathhouse. Flashes, confusing and dizzying. I see orange flames and golden sparks. There is smoke, and I see my hand, burned shiny and red. I can't tell the direction of the flames; my vision jumps around no matter how still I hold my head. Is the fire outside the window or inside the room? I can't tell.

I'm going to die, I realize. I can't escape. The flames will catch me eventually. I feel my legs buckle, and then I'm on the floor, crying. The pain in my hand grows, but it doesn't matter, since I'll soon be dead. All I see is fire, no matter where I look, and it is beautiful and terrifying. I haven't seen so much light since before I blinded myself. It's dazzling. Perhaps this is not the worst way to die.

I cough on a mouthful of smoke, my body fighting the inevitable. I should give up, I tell myself, but I can't fight the instinct that keeps screaming at me to run, to escape, no matter how impossible escape is. I hope the roof collapses. Then my death will be swift and relatively painless.

I hear a voice through the roar of the flames, someone calling out. "Thea!"

Hope fills me, and a surge of self-preservation overcomes me. "Here, I'm here," I shout back, though the smoke buffets my words around.

An eternity passes. I smell burning wood, cloth, and hair. My eyes weep from the smoke. My palm burns. I see nothing, the Sight long gone, and I leap when someone touches my arm.

"Thea, it's me, Timon."

I begin to cry, relief overcoming me. I reach out my arms like a small child asking for attention, and Timon lifts me up.

After several twists and turns and frightening waves of heat, Timon sets me down upon the grass, the smell of smoke still clinging to us. "Are you all right?" he asks, and his hands fumble with my body, checking my face, my arms, my feet. He sucks his breath in sharply when he sees my burned hand. "We need to get your hand in cold water," he says, though his voice carries a strain I'm not used to hearing. Is it fear? Regret? Guilt? Now that I am out of danger, my body wants to collapse, and my mind slugs painfully as I try to piece together what happened and what will be.

"It's just my hand," I say. "I'm all right."

Timon pulls me into an embrace, and my face is pressed against his chest. He smells so good underneath the smoke, cologne, and scented oils. I feel his heart hammering under my cheek, his hands shaking on my shoulders. The embrace is not the kind that an Eyes should offer his priestess, not at all deferential, not at all chaste.

"I thought I lost you," he says, pulling away, but his hands are still on my shoulders, his soft, aristocratic hands.

"I thought I was lost," I admit.

"Where is the amphora?" Timon asks.

"It was with my things."

I feel him pull away, cold air rushing to press against my skin. "I'll be back."

"No!" I shout and clutch for his hand, but my fingers slip through empty air. I hear him move across the garden toward the temple. I want to explain to him that it's just a jug. There's nothing special about it, certainly nothing special enough to risk his life. It was just a thing, just an object, and whether it had been touched by a god or not didn't change its significance.

A series of coughs wracks my body, my back arching. I spit up a wad of mucus from the back of my throat into the grass.

Coughing, I cry out for Timon, but he does not answer my calls.

Around me, I hear the fire roaring, the other priests leaving the temple. Someone cries out that the roof has caught; it's only a matter of time now before the temple is consumed. People are shouting, trying to contain the blaze, and others speculate about the cause. I can hardly believe that someone would set fire to a temple of blind priests, but the threat from the bathhouse repeats in my head. Whoever set the fire, did they really want the amphora, or was it set to hurt me?

Or Timon?

I feel a heavy shame. I should have left the amphora with the prince. I should have trusted my True Sight when it warned me every step of the journey. I should have told Timon the truth about the doubts in my faith. I should not have let him go.

I struggle to my feet and face the burning temple, the heat of the fire on my face. I see nothing, and, in that blindness, I take a measure of hope.

And Timon does come out, and I am told he is stained with

smoke but carries the amphora over his head with triumph. Later, physicians tell me that the scars will leave his face ruined, but he will otherwise recover. A miracle, they say, and I say it too. I sit by his side for weeks in the infirmary, and I tell him not to fear, for we will soon return to the temple of the blind, as has always been our fate.

The Graveyard Library

Anastasiya Sukhenko

Anastasiya Sukhenko is a writer and a self-taught photographer. Currently, she is an undergrad student at the University of South Florida majoring in psychology and minoring in creative writing. She has work published at For Women Who Roar®. You can find her on Instagram @anasukhenko.

The waiting hall was brightly lit from wide circle-top windows placed evenly on the ebony walls. The line for deliveries of books stretched down the entire room. Ella counted nearly a hundred people.

"I am sorry for your loss," the old woman said, taking a stack of parchment from a young man with bloodshot eyes and ink-stained hands. "The scribes will have it ready by the full moon."

From a marble bench, Ella watched the frail old woman add his writing to the collection of others behind her. Each stack of papers varied in height but shared smudges of carefully selected words and crinkled pages. The system seemed chaotic, and she worried if stories were ever crossed. *They're careful,* she reassured herself. *It would be cruel otherwise.* She continued to chew on the inside of her cheek as she waited to be invited inside the Library.

The next man in line pleaded to the old woman to accept another book from him. But the woman held up her bony hand and reminded him that he had already delivered three.

"Please...it's for my wife. She was taken during a raid," the man sobbed. "*Please.* The others...they were for my girls."

Ella bit her lip as she thought back to the night her village was raided. Forces from the opposing kingdom struck her village in the night. She had been one of few to survive. They had taken what they wanted, and they left her on the dirt road—perhaps thinking she had died. In many ways, she did.

Ella stood up from the waiting bench and crept up to the counter. "Excuse me, I want to offer up my shelf space for this man."

The old woman's raven eyes studied her. "You may. But you will only have—"

"He can have all of it."

The old woman's already shriveled face broke out a dozen more wrinkles as she scrutinized the girl. "Very well," she finally said. "Hand me your ticket."

Ella handed over her black stub. Sunlight from the windows shone down on the golden outline of a crescent moon: a seal to remind her of the only delivery she had—and ever will—make. As the woman's pale hand waved over the stub, it shimmered briefly before revealing two new crescents. The old woman returned Ella's ticket and briefly made note of this exchange in her logbook.

The man's mouth twitched as he searched for what to say. Ella gave him a half-smile, and as she began to walk away, he grabbed her hand. She flinched from his touch and pulled back.

"Sorry, I...I didn't mean to startle you. I just...I wanted to say *thank you*."

Ella could see the man was talking to her, but her mind was elsewhere—the putrid smell of burning oil paint, smoke blinding her, so much screaming...

"It's alright," Ella mumbled, pushing back the swarm of memories.

The creak from the large library doors echoed through the hall.

"Ella Lembrook," the bookkeeper announced. He was a short man, barely four feet tall, and had a long, peppered beard that fell to his belly.

Ella took a deep breath and approached the man, handing him her ticket.

He took out a gold monocle and examined the stub, focusing on the first crescent as if reading something only visible to him.

"Follow me," he prompted, placing the monocle and her stub in his coat pocket.

Stepping through the doors, Ella was greeted with ebony bookcases as high as the ceiling and a ceiling that reached as high as the sky. Each shelf was tightly packed with books bound in crimson, gold, and white buckram. The library was longer than the waiting hall, and she didn't have enough time to count the rows since the bookkeeper's stubby legs walked at an unnaturally brisk pace.

The gaps between the bookcases revealed glimpses of people speaking with their lost loved ones. One woman with auburn hair and a weathered face clutched onto the small hands of a little girl with the same sun-drenched locks. A few bookcases down was a girl with tearful brown eyes and ruddy cheeks leaning her head on the shoulder of a young man with a faint smile and closed eyes.

Ella could not tell which person was real or merely a phantom character from the books. *Perhaps, in some way they both are.*

There were very few crimson books but numerous gold ones. "What are the colors for?" Ella asked.

"The colors indicate the essence of the person. Red reminds us, bookkeepers, that the person could be hostile due to the nature of the writing. Occasionally, someone will include how the person died. Seldom is it a peaceful death. Many are from the war and those that live close to the battles died from the raids," the bookkeeper said, taking a sharp left and leading them down another aisle. "A book bound in gold indicates an understanding, amicable person. The writing has a balance of good and bad remembrances. In some cases, the story mentions that the person died, but the details are omitted."

They made another left. *This place is endless*, Ella thought.

"White means the person does not realize they are dead," the bookkeeper continued. "They might not even know who or what they truly are. They might feel lost, disoriented. Often these books are of young children, even infants. Parents will exclude bad memories or create new ones. All of which might limit the development of a whole person. They could just be fragments of a person or an entirely new person is formed."

"You call them people, not characters," Ella mentioned. "Does that mean you think they're real?"

"A curious question. I think they are as real as we believe anything to be. One could argue they are *more* real than you and I."

"You truly believe that?"

"Do you not? Our bodies die, decay. But our stories, well, they live on."

Ella took comfort in his belief.

"Lembrook...Ah, here," the bookkeeper said. He flicked his hand and a white book floated downward. Engraved in black letters on the book's spine was E. *Lembrook.*

"How *curious*," he remarked, handing her the lofty book.

Ella held it timidly. "How...does it work?"

"Open it to a page that brings out the most emotion. Read it aloud, quietly. Once you are finished, close the book and bring it to me or another bookkeeper near the entrance. You will be handed back your ticket. You are allowed one appointment per month. Relish this visit." Before he turned away, he added, "Remember, they cannot form new memories. Whatever you say here and now will be forgotten the moment you close the book."

Ella brushed her fingers across the shimmering white cover. She took a seat against the bookcase. There seemed to be a hundred books on a single shelf. She opened hers to the first page. It wasn't her handwriting, but it was her words. The scribes had turned her messy scrawls into a cohesive cursive work. She traced her fingers over the beautiful penmanship and wondered how their magic worked. Did the scribes' hands permanently ache from rewriting everyone's deliveries? Maybe their magic prevented that. The scribes' method was as much a mystery to her as it was to everyone else.

Ella flipped through pages until she finally stopped on the one that she had rewritten too many times. The night her village was raided.

"It was a terribly hot evening, but that was the only flaw of that night. You saw from the moonlight your paintings scattered around your cottage. You were so proud of each one," Ella said, taking a deep breath to ease the knot in her throat. "You thought you'd never finish, but you did. All the coin and hours you spent would be rewarded. Tomorrow you were going to present them to the gallery. You fell asleep to the sound of Misty's purring and Theo's arm around you."

"I loved that night," a mousy voice said.

Startled, Ella turned to see a stranger with all the same features as herself. The same matted blonde hair, deep brown eyes, and a round face. Only, this girl was lighter in her speech, and she smiled fully and genuinely.

This is mad, Ella thought, eyeing the girl in front of her.

The girl turned to her, grasping the situation, her expression confused.

Ella searched for what to say. She had prepared for this, but all of it escaped her. "I...I can't believe I'm meeting you."

"I don't understand," the girl replied, giving a nervous laugh. Ella's laugh. "You're me..."

"I am. And I'm not," Ella began. She swallowed the knot in her throat and peered at the book. "You're who I wanted to be."

A few tears dampened the page.

The girl put her hand on Ella's shoulder. Ella laughed slightly. *This is absurd. All of it.*

"Why are you crying?" the girl asked.

Ella didn't know how to answer that. Not simply, at least.

"It doesn't matter," Ella said, wiping away her tears. She hesitated. "Tell me about...our life. It'll make me feel better."

"Our life?" the girl thought for a moment. "Hmm...We grew up in Bellwick. It was a small village. *Too* small. Our mom and dad are farmers, but Mom's parents were poets. So, Mom used to read to us. She taught us how to read and write and we *hated* it. Um...oh! On our eighth birthday, Dad bought us a paint set. That was the *best* day," the girl said, grinning. "Our best friend Theo lived in the house next to us. His cat, Patches, had babies and he gave us Misty. *A lot* of our paintings were of Misty," the girl laughed.

Ella smiled at that truth.

"We're married to Theo," the girl continued. "Everyone thought we were too young. But they were wrong. Now we live in Silentvale and our paintings are displayed in the gallery! We couldn't believe it..."

Ella stared at the girl as if she were a mirror. Only this mirror reflected the life she had only ever seen in her mind. The knot in her throat grew tighter.

"What did you mean when you said I'm 'who you wanted to be'?" the girl asked.

"You won't like what I tell you," Ella admitted. *But you won't remember anyway.* "The life you have...it's not real. Not entirely. It's the life I always imagined for myself. The life I always wanted."

"Then," the girl hesitated. "I'm not real?"

Ella thought back to what the bookkeeper had said. "You are. In a way. This story—*your story*—is the one that'll be remembered."

"It's not your story too?"

Ella shook her head.

"In my story, Mom never read to me and Dad didn't buy me a paint set. *I* bought myself a paint set with what I saved. I had to hide it at Theo's house. Misty was real, and the paintings, but I never married Theo." Ella took a deep breath. "He died after he was drafted in the war...so did Dad. Mom got sick and died too. I would've been entirely alone if it wasn't for Misty." She clutched onto the book. "I never lived in Silentvale. But there was a contest for the gallery, and I entered. The night before I was supposed to leave...there was a raid. All of Bellwick was burned down. Misty...she died too..." Ella could barely get her words out. "I lost everything..."

Tears fell from the girl. She was experiencing only an echo of the pain Ella felt.

"You won't remember what I told you," Ella reassured. "You'll forget once I leave. But your life will be more real than mine. *You* will be remembered as Ella Lembrook."

The girl was trying to piece it all together. "What about you?"

"Now, I can leave. Leave this life behind...as if it never existed."

"Leave? And go where?"

"Wherever you go after life."

"What!? No. You can't do that to yourself!" the girl protested.

"I can. I didn't get to choose the life I started with, but I can choose when I want it to end—"

"That's not right—"

"People die every day, and they don't always get to choose how or when. People are *forgotten* every day. I've already decided, and you know how stubborn we are. In this one way, I'm lucky. I get to rewrite my story."

The girl sat with Ella in silence.

"Tell me your favorite memory," Ella finally said.

The girl glanced at Ella regrettably. She took a deep breath. "My favorite memory...is my first kiss with Theo. By the lavender fields. He thought it would be sweet, but I'm allergic to lavender and I kept sneezing." The girl laughed. "He held my hand the entire night. That was the night he promised to marry me."

Ella smiled, thinking back on that moment.

"Was that real?" the girl asked.

Ella took one final look at herself. "It was," she said, and closed the book.

Little, Little, Little

K. A. Tutin

K. A. Tutin is a writer whose work has also appeared in Syntax and Salt, Every Day Fiction, and Flash Fiction Magazine.

The crows call you Little.

They must have chosen the name because of how small you are, curled up into a tight ball, a tiny speck against the white. You accept the name as yours because you don't know if you have another.

You listen to their squawking voices, wet and muffled against the snow. The tree branches creak when the crows settle to feed, clustered together as matted feathers and clawed feet, gnawing at the bark to pluck out the beetles that burrow there. They study you, with insects pinched between their stubbed bills, as though they wonder how you arrived here. You can't answer that question, just as you don't know your name. But you know some things. There had been walking, then darkness, and light, before you awoke in the murky forest with the crows poking at your shivering and naked body, combing through your hair to ease out the tangled leaves.

"Come, Little," they say, echoing in the shadowed trees. "Little, Little, Little."

You unstick your lip from your dry gums. "Why?" you ask, throat raw.

The crows peel away from the branches, disappearing above, and you force yourself onto your feet. Snow crunches under your toes, sticks stabbing your bare feet. You keep walking even as the rising sun burns your eyes and the aching in your body sinks to bone. You walk until the trees become sparse and open out to an empty corner road, where a cottage sits on the opposite side. Smoke wafts from the chimney, the wooden wind chimes hanging from the porch clacking together in the wind. Your hands hurt when you wrap your fingers around the door handle and push it open.

You notice the heat from the fireplace first, and hurry to sit in front of it. Feeling returns to your hands, flushing your pale skin and easing the tension in your jaw enough to unclench it. The living room is cosy, with the mellow yellow walls and blue-knitted rugs, blankets thrown across a suede sofa, and trinkets cluttering the many shelves. You sit on the sofa, welcoming the change from gritty snow.

One of the crows sits on the window sill outside. It studies you and waits. You know it waits for you. Why does it wait for you? Why don't you follow it?

You look away when the door opens again and a woman walks in with logs bundled in her arms. She wears round, chained glasses on the end of her nose, and her cheeks are flushed and spider-webbed with spindly veins.

She stops stamping her boots for a moment to look at you. "What are you doing?" she asks. "Who are you?"

You flex your tingling fingers. "I'm cold."

The woman comes closer. Her eyes widen. "You're a child."

"My name is Little," you say, because you can't think of anything else.

She drops the firewood and flicks on the light. A warm glow basks the room. "Have you been outside long?"

You shrug. "I woke up in the snow."

"Right." She drags her hand through her hair, then grabs one of the scratchy blankets, throwing it over your damp shoulders. "You've been like this the whole time? Naked?" You shrug again, and the woman crouches down in front of you, knees popping. "Did someone leave you out there?" You frown. She tries again. "Are you lost?"

Something tells you that it is not exactly true, but it feels familiar enough to be the closest thing to right. You nod.

The woman stands, vanishing into the kitchen. She returns a moment later with a steaming mug, and places it in your hands, encouraging you to take a sip. You taste chocolate, as warm as the fire beside you. When the woman busies around with putting the wood in the fireplace and pacing with labored breaths, you stay seated, looking out the window. The crow has gone. Coldness dowses over you. You don't look away until you're sure the crow won't return, when the sky bleeds orange.

You feel a prickling in your thigh, rubbing against the blanket. You pull it back. A tiny fleck of black pokes out from your skin. You pinch it and tug, wincing at the sting. You stare at the feather in your hand, its root stained wet with your blood.

Hope swoops within you. Maybe the crows have not left you after all.

***

You're standing in the downstairs hallway when you overhear the woman talking in the kitchen. Morning light cuts through the blinds, shards across the marble tiles. She gave you old pyjamas to wear, not telling you where they came from, along with another serving of hot chocolate, which you now cradle against your chest even though it has gone cold overnight.

"—supposed to know that she'll be taken care of? What if no one comes for her?" the woman says, voice rough around the edges. "What would you do, Paula?"

A kettle whistles and a chair scrapes, drowning out the rest of her words. You peer around the corner. The woman is washed out, with bloodshot eyes and fingernails chewed down to the quick, looking as though she has not slept. Something unpleasant roils in your stomach, making you step out into full view and edge toward her, hand outstretched. She startles when you stop beside her, and she opens her mouth, but then stops, her red-ringed gaze dropping down to your thigh. You had picked the fabric apart until it peeled and revealed your weeping skin, swollen with a new clump of feathers. A soft coat that shines iridescent under the light.

She reaches out and encircles your wrist, gentle, comforting. "What happened?"

"I don't know," you say, and miss her touch when she lets go of you.

She studies your thigh a moment later, then nods. "Okay," she says. "You're going to stay here with me. Until we find you a home."

With your third mug of hot chocolate, stomach growing heavy and sloshy, you go to your borrowed room. The woman seemed reluctant to give it to you, telling you not to touch anything. Last night you kept your hands to yourself, staying away from the picture books about space on the shelves and dolls on the dresser. You grab one of the blankets the woman laid out for you, and wrap it around yourself as you sit by the window.

Snow melts against the glass, blurring the bare and gnarled trees that shudder in the distance. The crows sit on the sill, preening their flake-covered feathers. Not one of them speaks to you this time. The one from the day before, larger and bill crooked, stares at your thigh. You down at the rest of your hot chocolate until only the dregs remain. As you rest your head against the window and watch the crows, you imagine yourself flying among them.

***

You wake at dawn to find the feathers continuing to grow, sleek as they bloom across your leg. Your first thought, aside from the crows, is to show the woman their progress.

The cottage is quiet and empty, save for the creaking as it settles. You spot the woman outside, standing alone and staring ahead. An axe dangles from her fingers, chopped logs scattered around her feet. She seems to shake herself and returns to her work, heaving groans each time she brings the blade down.

Once more you feel that uncomfortable feeling in your stomach. You turn away and head back to the kitchen, grabbing a mug and hot chocolate sachet from the cupboards you barely manage to reach on your tiptoes. You pour the water in from the kettle, and stir the thick mixture, mimicking the same way the woman has done it all those times for you. A twig snaps beneath you as you step outside, causing the woman to flinch. She relaxes when she sees it's you, and when you hold the mug out, her eyebrows raise. She takes it anyway.

She takes a sip. "It's cold," she says. She forces a smile. "But that's okay—"

You do it without thinking: you pluck out one of your feathers. You wipe away the blood and offer it to her.

The woman hesitates before reaching out, quiet. You smile, something rusty from the way it slopes, as her fingers close around it.

She looks up at you with watery eyes. "Thank you," she whispers, then: "Excuse me."

When she walks away, you stare at her back, chest sinking, before returning to your room, where the crows wait for you. Somehow they have opened the window a crack, slipping inside. They sit on your leg. They preen at your feathers with their bills, soothing enough to ease the sadness that threatens to overwhelm you. "Little," they say in their symphony of cawing voices. "Come."

The last time you had asked them why, but it had felt more like instinct than conscious questioning. A vague hesitation stirs within you. Do you truly want to go with the crows, or do you want to stay? The crows and the woman both welcomed you with open wings and arms. How can you choose between their kindness? Do either of them truly want the same? You press your hand into your feathers, scrunching them in your fist, and ask them again, "Why?"

They ruffle their coats. The one with its crooked bill speaks. "Need us," it says. "With us."

When they leave, you watch them go, disappearing into the dense trees, their voices drifting until they become an echo.

You straddle the threshold between here and there, and the question of whether to step back or forward stays with you as you lie back on the pillows. You try to imagine yourself flying among them, but another image pushes alongside: you sit at the woman's kitchen table, talking with her, while you drink hot chocolate.

***

Throughout the days and nights that follow, you continue to transform. You shorten by five inches, unable to reach the hot chocolate sachets even when you stand on a stool. Your nose has sharped into a point, your tongue slimming and darkening. And your hands widen and blacken, like the shadows that dance across the ground as you dig into the slushy snow.

The woman comes over to you. She has seemed to have since forgotten the incident where you gave her one of your feathers. "Little," she says, wiping her hands on her floral apron. "What are you doing?"

Leaves knot in your hair as you crawl out from the bushes, twigs scraping against your skin. "Food," you say, and hold out a fist clenched around a wriggling, sodden-earthed worm.

She tuts and wipes your hands. "Wash it down with this." She hands you a mug. The one you always ask for: chipped rim, with sparrows patterned over the porcelain.

You drink as much as your bill allows. A leaf falls down from your hair into your mug.

Something flickers over the woman's face, as though torn with a decision, before she holds out her hand. "Want me to take care of that for you?"

You nod and take her hand, where she guides you over to the back door step. She goes inside and then returns with a comb, and crouches down behind you. Your scalp stings at the first pass, plastic teeth crunching as they catch on the knots. Once the passes become soft and comforting, you think about how the woman's gentle touches remind you of the crows, how they had smoothed the damp tangles and tweezed out the twigs and leaves as you lay back in the forest and stared up at the sky. You lean back until you rest against the woman's chest and ask, "Who is Paula?"

Wind rustles the trees and whistles between the branches as the moment stills. "She is—" the woman pauses. "She was my daughter."

"What happened to her?" you ask, looking over your shoulder in time to see the woman briefly close her eyes and take a deep breath.

"She died, a long time ago," she says, and nothing more on the matter. The next pause is long and bloated, and her voice cracks when she speaks again. "She liked to have her hair brushed."

You lean into her hand as she runs it through your hair, then turn around to face her. You have no hot chocolate, and she already has one of your feathers, so you reach out and take her hand instead, lacing your fingers together.

She brushes her thumb over your knuckles, where bristles grow, and gives you a fleeting smile that wavers at the corners. "You watch the crows," she says, and tucks a strand behind your ear, pausing to cradle your chin. "You can go with them, or you can stay here with me. Either place can be your home."

The crows have been watching you from the trees since this morning, even pointing you in the direction of where to find the best worms. You stare down at your empty mug, tasting the remnant of sweetness on your tongue. Both the crows and the woman care for you, which makes it all the more difficult to know where you want to be. You sigh and say, "I don't know."

"You could do both, or neither, or something else entirely," she says, "but don't stay still when you could be moving."

You keep your hand laced with hers, but turn away and watch the sunset. Hush washes over you both, leaving you with only your breaths to listen to.

***

You change when snow has fallen.

The woman kneels beside your bed when she finds you that way, taller and louder. In her front pocket is the feather you gave her. She holds out her shaking hand and takes you into her cupped palm. You nip at her thumb, leaning into her touch when she brushes down your spine. You both linger for a while more, before she reaches past and unlatches the window, swinging it open. A biting wind gusts over you, but you jump onto the sill and wait.

"Are you ready?" she asks, and waits for your answer, along with the crows from where they perch in the trees. You cannot choose.

Some part of you believes that you will never be ready for what paths may come, but another part of you believes that those paths were made for you to follow. How could you be ready when you do not know what lies ahead? What you can be ready for is finding out, because you cannot have the journey without discovery.

You hop forward, leaving imprints of your claws behind, and open your wings. The crows watch you, and the woman watches you, something open and bittersweet. You follow the urge to beat your wings, taking off into the pink dusk. You leave the woman, but you don't fly toward the crows. Perhaps one day you will return for another hot chocolate, and perhaps one day you will fly with them, but today you will seek out yourself.

Today you soar alone, high into the sky, where it welcomes your arrival.

The Adopt a Zombie Program

Sophia Thimmes

Sophia Thimmes has a thing for stories, forests, and carb-based food products. She studies creative writing at Utah State University where she stares wistfully at the mountains a lot. Her writing has appeared in Sink Hollow, The Ekphrastic Review, and of course, Luna Station Quarterly.

I stared at them through the thick glass. They really were sort of cute. Their skin clung tight to their small skulls, which made their distant eyes appear large as foreign planets set afloat in a sky of mottled flesh. Dresses adorned with lace and tiny printed flowers swayed as they paced in their separate enclosures.

I pulled out my cell phone and took a quick video clip of a pacing child zombie and then decorated the footage with sparkling heart emojis before adding it to my story. After sliding my phone into my back pocket, I tapped once on the glass. The girl within swiveled her head toward me, and I jolted back. Long, dark hair framed a pale face with silvery scars.

"Oh well, isn't she a sweet thing! What's her name?" My mom leaned towards the paper description pasted to the upper corner of the glass and tucked a brown curl behind her ear when it fell forward. "*Abigail.* How sweet! Likes Barbie Dolls and good with cats. Minimal scarring and bruising. 8 years old. All immunizations up to date and looking for a forever home. What do you think, John?"

"Seems like she would be a great fit for us," Dad said, eager to get the adoption process over with, having looked at zombies all morning. "All of these zombies are starting to *bleed together,*"

Dad said to me with a wink that looked more like a full-face scrunch. He chuckled at his own joke until he looked back up at the glass and jumped. Abigail was much closer to the glass than she had been a moment before. Dad coughed.

My mom gave a sharp laugh. "Oh shush, none of them have any open wounds. What do you think, Rebecca?"

I looked back at the zombie. I liked having a cat. I figured it couldn't be that different.

"Really cute," I said. I just wanted to make it back home in time to meet up with Mackenzie and still get to the party we were going to at the ideal 30-45 minutes late mark.

My mom waved over an employee who got a leash for Abigail, droned on about care instructions, and gave the mandatory safety explanations. I zoned out, having already heard all this stuff in school.

Once the vaccine came out that made the public immune and the already-turned harmless, people didn't know what to do with all of the vacant-eyed humans that roamed the streets like purpling dolls. The vaccine, along with the brain damage caused by the virus, made them completely docile, and their physical development stopped at the age they had been infected. Some people liked to shoot them for sport out of their trucks. Some people used them for perverted means. Others, like my mom, argued violence against zombies was inhumane and should be considered abuse. For many, it seemed strange to hurt something so humanoid and complacent. Several zombie rights activists began campaigning for better treatment of zombies, which led to the Zombie Justice Act several years ago. Of course, with so many crowding the shelters, some still had to be put down—something the zombie pet commercials emphasized as melancholic music swelled in the background. Commercials with trendy celebrities emphatically reciting lines such as:

Totally safe, totally adorable.

I lost a child to the Outbreak, but now I can provide the home I wish my lost zombie child had.

Zombies. The modern pet for the modern family.

On the drive back from the pet store, my mom twisted around in the passenger seat to coo at Abigail as we drove through suburban neighborhoods. Abigail sat a seat apart from me, blinking her planet eyes. Once we arrived in the driveway, my mom, leash in hand, led Abigail through the front door and into our living room where Ida, our cat, hissed upon seeing the new addition to our family and arched her grey back.

"There, there, Ida, we'll still have plenty of attention for you," my mom said. "It'll just take some getting used to." Whether she was talking to the cat, Dad and I, Abigail, or herself was unclear.

In a week's time, we settled into a routine. Mom fed her. I walked her. Dad would tie her to the stair rail in the evenings. Zombies don't sleep, so at night Abigail was given a chair to sit on and her leash knotted around the wooden railing that led up to my parents' bedroom ("So she doesn't hurt herself," my mom had said).

If I got up for a glass of water or a small stack of Oreos in the night, she would regard me with eyes that glinted black in the darkness as I made my way across the living room to the kitchen. On my way back to my bedroom, they would track me once again.

"Hey there, Abigail," I would say, around a mouthful of Oreos. Abigail would blink back at me. I was never sure how much she understood.

My mom loved to brush Abigail's long, dark hair and braid it into elaborate hairstyles. When I arrived home from school, the two of them would often be sat in front of the TV, the suspenseful music of a cooking or dating game show coming from the speakers, as my mom's fingers disappeared and reappeared in the swathes of Abigail's hair like worms rippling through mud. I had never had the patience to sit still for so long when I was Abigail's age.

"There's my pretty girl," my mom would say as she admired her own handiwork then turned to a metallic tin overflowing with shimmering polishes. After selecting some glooping, glimmering color, she would unscrew the top, pick up one of Abigail's small, shriveled hands and begin painting her tiny, yellowing nails. The whole living room would thicken with a toxic aroma.

Abigail didn't smell bad, exactly. She smelled synthetic. Before we had adopted her, she had been doused in some sort of preservative and then perfumed with something that smelled strongly of bubblegum. My mom kept Abigail in a continual fog of sugary fragrance and hairspray.

"Would you like to join us?" my mom would ask.

"Uh, no thanks, I have homework," I would say as I escaped to my bedroom.

One evening, after giving up on a math problem set, I laid back on my fluffy blue comforter and called Mackenzie. Mackenzie had perfect, tight ringlets, a pool, and the expert ability to find indie bands just before they got big.

"We got a zombie," I said as I stared at the cluttered shelves that flanked my walls. Two Barbies remained from my old collection, and they observed my messy room from above with cool expressions, their shadowed eyelids drawn halfway down. Surrounding their tiny plastic bodies were band aid wrappers from when I had cut my ankle shaving, a congealed mac and cheese bowl, a large pocketknife that I had used to carve my name into a park picnic table, and a collection of band pins from the local shows Mackenzie had taken me along to.

"You did? Like in the commercials?"

"Yeah."

"Cool. I was obsessed with them back in middle school, but my parents never let me get one."

"Why not?"

"They were paranoid that the drugs they give the zombies after the vaccine would eventually stop working."

"You have to give them drugs?" I pictured Abigail, in her pretty pink dress, snorting cocaine off the coffee table, my mom having carefully placed it into a neat little row for her beforehand.

"Yeah, they like, keep them really sedated or something? You're the one with the zombie, Becca. Shouldn't you know this?"

I had only gotten a C- on the exam we took at the end of our zombie unit last year in school, and I hadn't been listening to the employee at the pet store when he had started rambling about care instructions. I had been staring at a still, blue fish in a clouded tank wondering if it was dead or not.

The next morning was a Saturday, and I spent an hour in bed on QuikPiks scrolling through posts. A selfie of Mackenzie with her neck tilted to one side, her mouth open, a guitar in her lap. A cake in the shape of a kitten. Suicide memes that I had already seen.

The icon for a suggested account caught my eye. The image was small, but the two figures it featured looked familiar. Was it my mom and Abigail? I clicked on the username, ZomMom. Column after column of photos featuring my mom and Abigail appeared on the screen. My mom and Abigail poised with dainty floral tea-cups in hand, Abigail's overflowing with the pink and red slop she ate. My mom and Abigail in front of our garden, matching flower crowns on their heads. The back of Abigail's head with a big heart braided into it. A clip of my mom saying, "play dead!" and Abigail reclining on the sofa in our living room with her eyes closed. I scrolled back up to the follower count. 11k.

I put my phone down. I felt oddly like I was intruding on something.

***

Since I was the one tasked with walking her, and Dad was the one tasked with spending time with me, walking Abigail became our father/daughter time. Every evening, or nearly every, Dad and I would make our rounds around the neighborhood, past the well-manicured lawns and the park with a small, glimmer-ing pond. Abigail would walk on the pavement in front of us, a beacon guiding the way in her bright dress.

"Is it just me or is Mom kind of weird about Abigail?" I said as we made our way past the pond. Abigail's back seemed to straighten slightly at the mention of her name.

"Eh, it's a hobby. She's a caring person. You should have seen her with you when you were younger!" Dad said.

"I wasn't a pet, though."

"Well, you sure did act like an animal sometimes!"

I didn't laugh.

Dad sighed. "You know, during the Outbreak, your mom was terrified of losing you. You were only six, and you got sick so often."

"So? I'm still here."

"You are." Dad smiled at me and rumpled my hair, which I was quick to smooth back into place with my free hand.

Dad looked down at his feet and furrowed his brow. "I think there's something comforting for her in holding death so close and feeling like she can control it. You know, the thing that could have taken you away from us."

There's something comforting for her in holding death so close and feeling like she can control it. That sounded like lyrics to some song that Mackenzie would listen to.

I didn't see what the issue was. The Outbreak had been years ago, and I was fine.

"Is it true that all zombie pets are on drugs?" I asked.

"It's like the pet store employee said, you give them drugs to keep them calm."

"Doesn't the vaccine do that?"

"Think of it like insurance, Becca."

The concept of insurance had always been slightly confusing to me. I thought of the mornings that I had watched my mom crush up white pills and sprinkle them over Abigail's bowl of slop. When I had asked her what they were for, she had said that it was Abigail's medicine to keep her happy and healthy. When I had asked her if they were like vitamins she replied, "sort of," as she kissed the top of my head. I had squirmed from beneath her touch.

The leash was suddenly tugged from my grip as Abigail bolted to a nearby tree and crouched down low.

"Abigail!" Dad called as he jogged over to her huddled form.

Abigail rose, the legs and bushy tail of a squirrel dangling from her mouth. Her white Peter Pan collar was sprayed with blood.

***

"Abigail ate a squirrel on our walk," I told Mom after I had made it back home and upstairs to her bedroom.

"Hm, yes, she brings me things sometimes," my mom said. She reclined on her throw pillows with her long, smooth legs thrown out and shining atop the comforter. I imagined the feathery carcasses of small birds and the blood-stained fur of rodents tossed onto her white bedding like roses. "It's quite sweet, but I have to bleach the stains out of her dresses afterwards."

"I found your QuikPiks account," I said. It came out more like an accusation than I had meant it.

"Oh, do you like it? It's a fun hobby."

"You have a lot of followers."

"We're starting to get sponsorships. I got several eyeshadow palettes in the mail for free today. Isn't that nice?"

"Very nice," I said and left the room.

***

That night, I awoke to a wet, chewing sound. Rolling over, as my eyes adjusted to the darkness, I saw Abigail in the corner of my room with the head of one of my Barbie dolls in her mouth, her teeth grinding away at Barbie's shiny, plastic hair and causing the small head to deflate again and again with each bite.

I let out a shrill cry. Abigail continued chomping away at the Barbie, completely unbothered by my scream. I heard the rapid thud of footsteps on the stairs.

"What's wrong?" my mom said as the door to my bedroom was slammed open and the bodies of my parents crammed in the doorway.

My mom flipped on the light switch, and my parents followed my pointing finger across the clothes-strewn carpet to where Abigail was crouched in the corner. The sound of plastic being chewed squelched from her mouth. A doll eating a doll. A torn red leash hung from her neck like a ribbon. I watched the tension ooze from my mom's shoulders like nail polish spilling across a coffee table from a toppled bottle.

My mom rubbed her eyes. She looked fragile in her pale, silk nightdress. "Honey, did you forget to feed her?"

I thought back to earlier that evening. Homework. Mackenzie on the phone. Had Mom asked me to feed her? She had.

"Come on Abby girl, let's go get you something to eat. Honey, be a little more careful next time. Plastic isn't good for zombies," Mom said as she trod across my discarded clothes to scoop up Abigail's thin body as if it were a bundle of sticks bound by taffeta and crinoline. "And please clean up your room tomorrow. You'll get spiders." The dark hair of my mom and Abigail mingled at their shoulders and made them look like a strange, two-headed beast as they left the room with Dad in tow.

The lone Barbie left on my shelf looked accusingly at me as if to say, *It's your fault I'm up here all alone now. How could you let this happen?*

I pushed my bookcase and the chest that I kept at the foot of my bed in front of my door before climbing back into bed, even though it made me feel silly to be afraid of something so much smaller than me. Something that wore frilly, flower-printed dresses.

***

The next night, after staying up late watching short documentaries about alleged alien sightings online, I got out of bed for my usual small stack of Oreos. When I opened my bedroom door, I could see Abigail sitting still with her hands on her lap by the stair rail. Her small, pale face was framed by two long pigtails which had been lovingly secured by my mom. She had a new leash—purple this time. Her blank eyes met mine from across the room.

I'm going to eat you, I imagined her saying. *They don't need you anymore. Maybe I'll eat them too. I'm so, so hungry, Rebecca.*

I shut my door and placed my furniture in front of it again.

***

"Dad, have you seen Ida around lately?" I asked one morning.

"Uh-huh, Honey," Dad said as he took a bite of his tomato bagel sandwich and stared out the window.

"When?"

Dad glanced away from the window. Crumbs flecked his mouth.

"Sorry, what?"

"Dad. *Ida*. Have you seen her around?"

Dad made his scrunched-up thinking face as he chewed. "I haven't. Why?"

"Her food and water bowl has been full since yesterday morning. You didn't refill them, did you?"

"No, but I'm sure she'll turn up. Isn't that what cats do? Wander around and then come back?"

Maybe, but Ida had never been gone for more than a day before.

***

When I got home from school, Ida's food and water bowl was still full and the sink was full of dishes congealed with pink meat slop. I made my way through the living room and ran up the stairs to my parents' bedroom. I knocked hard on the door before throwing it open.

Mom was laying on top of the covers in a sheer pink robe lined with pink fur. Her eyes were closed, and her mouth hung open. The curls of her dark hair were fanned out over a pale pillowcase. Abigail sat on the bed beside her, her back hunched slightly, as she gnawed on a lock of my mom's hair.

"Mom!" I shouted.

My mom jolted awake and sat up, blinking and looking disgruntled. The lock of her hair fell away from Abigail's mouth.

"What is it?"

"Abigail was eating your hair."

My mom looked back at Abigail. She laughed as she tucked a stray hair of Abigail's away. "Oh. Your dad and I had a puppy in college that used to do that all the time."

"Abigail is *not* a puppy."

My mom straightened the shoulders of her robe and tied the silk sash at her waist.

"No, of course not."

"Mom, where's Ida?"

"Ida?" My mom got up and took Abigail's hand as she guided her off the bed.

"I haven't seen her in two days."

"Oh, well, I'm sure she'll turn up." My mom began making the bed, running her fingers along the blankets and smoothing out all the little creases.

"Yeah, when Abigail drops her bloody carcass at your feet?"

My mom began arranging the throw pillows with aggression, her movements harsh and jerky. "Rebecca. If Ida doesn't turn up, we'll all put up posters. Cats wander all the time. I'm sure we'll find her. You know that Abigail would never kill a cat. Ida would be far too big for her little mouth."

"She was eating your hair!"

"Just what exactly are you implying, Rebecca?" My mom stopped what she was doing to stare hard at me.

"That you should be more careful with her!"

"Good grief, Rebecca, look at her!" my mom gestured to Rebecca, who stood straight up in her yellow dress like a doll waiting to be taken down from a shelf and played with. Did I imagine an amused glimmer pass over her features? A slight upward tug at the corner of her mouth? "I've napped with Abigail around before. You're being paranoid."

"I'm not being paranoid, you're being delusional!"

"*Rebecca.* I've done my research! I would never place you or your dad in danger like that!"

I scoffed.

"I'm the one who's parented you for the last 14 years. You could give me some credit, you know." My mom pinched the bridge of her nose.

"I was never a zombie!"

"But if you had been, we would have found a way—" my mom began walking toward me.

I left the room and slammed the door behind me.

***

A couple of days later, after lying awake for hours, I grabbed my phone from off the bedside table and opened QuikPiks. A post from ZomMom was at the top. I had been avoiding it, but now I clicked on the account page.

A picture of Abigail posed on our floral couch in a yellow dress with rain falling outside of the window behind her. The caption: *Rainy Days call for bright dresses* :). A closeup of Abigail's face, her scars smoothed by a thick layer of concealer and her eyelids powdered to a glittering gold gradient. The caption: *Had so much fun creating this look for my sweet Abby. It's almost as sparkly as her personality! (Sponsored by BoldlyBright Cosmetics).* A clip of my mom telling Abigail to sit and Abigail squashing her fluffy red tutu on a chair as she obeyed. The account's follower count was up to 12k.

I clicked on ZomMom's story that featured a linked article titled "How Drugging Your Zombie Pet is Causing Them Harm." My mom had added text around the link that read, "Such important information!! Wish more people knew about this :(I know that Abigail would NEVER hurt anybody." I clicked on the link and scanned the article. There were comparisons between giving your zombie pet pills and encouraging your child to do drugs. There were promises that if you gave up feeding your zombie pet their pills, they would start to seem "livelier" and "happier." The article ended with statements about how incidents resulting in harm were *"very uncommon."* I couldn't find any citations. So, this was the research my mom had been doing. I put my phone down.

Abigail's squirrel and Barbie meals must have been examples of "liveliness."

My eyes found the spot at the end of my bed where Ida sometimes liked to curl up after nosing her way into my room. She still hadn't turned up.

I glanced at the dark silhouette of the lone Barbie on my shelf. She looked like a fallen angel. *Well, what now, Rebecca? Are you too afraid of Little Miss Roadkill to do anything?*

I threw back my covers and grabbed the pocketknife from off my shelf before opening my bedroom door. I didn't want to turn on the lights just in case my parents would notice, so I walked over to Abigail's shadowy form in the dark. I placed my pocketknife between my teeth as I untied Abigail's leash from the railing. After I had finally untangled all of Dad's knots, I slowly opened the front door and led her out into the night, past the shadowed suburban two-stories, past the darkened pond, and past the little bikes laying, in trust, on the otherwise neat lawns.

Our neighborhood was a quiet one, and we were the only ones out. This left all of my attention for Abigail. I kept glancing at her sideways, the fingers of one hand coiled tightly around the new leash, and the fingers of the other coiled tightly around the pocketknife. I kept expecting her to make a dash towards a wandering cat, a fluffy-tailed squirrel, my face, but she only stared straight ahead in silence as we walked along the sidewalk.

Mackenzie's house loomed before us. All the windows were dark. I led Abigail to the side of the house and reached over a low gate to undo the latch. We made our way into the backyard that was fringed by a white fence and tidy shrubs. The pool was in the center. I pulled back the cover. The surface rippled as the sharp tang of chlorine filled the air, reminding me of all the summers I had spent here with Mackenzie, eating popsicles and sharing a humongous inflated flamingo. I brought Abigail to the edge of the pool.

"Sit, Abigail," I said.

Her small body squatted down, and she jutted her legs over the rim of the pool, soaking the sparkling, lavender tights that hid the green and yellow bruises that mottled her legs. Her Mary Janes loomed below like two black fish oddly distorted by the water. This end of the pool was eight feet deep—more than plenty to cover her short body. If she had learned to swim before she had been infected with the virus, would the muscle memory remain now? I looked at her tiny form. The drooping hairbow, the narrow shoulders, the downcast head. Was I wrong? Was Abigail as harmless as my mom thought, and would Ida be waiting for me to let her in once I got back home? I thought of Abigail's white collar flecked with blood. *She brings me things sometimes.*

"Abigail, play dead."

Abigail laid back on the concrete and closed her eyes.

I crouched down and pushed until Abigail's torso was parallel to the edge of the pool. Her clothing snagged slightly on the concrete, and I wondered if I was scraping her cheek. I gave her a shove and watched her topple into the water with a splash. She sank down, down, and then bobbed, facedown, to the surface with her top and skirt inflating with water. I stood with my heart thudding in my chest for what felt like forever, but Abigail didn't make a move. She just remained suspended in the water like some ridiculously outfitted animal preserved in formaldehyde. I glanced up anxiously at the windows of Mackenzie's house, but they all remained dark.

When finally I thought enough time had passed, I put the pool cover back in place over the top of Abigail and crept quickly back to the fence. Even the soft sound of my sneakers on the grass made me wince. Once I was on the other side of the gate, I finally started to feel a sense of relief that neared euphoria. As I made sure the latch was in place, I glanced one more time at the side of the pool that was still visible. I could see the lump of Abigail's body just beneath the pool cover.

How would my mom let her followers know?

A photo of Abigail face down in the pool with her dark hair floating outwards. Caption: *So sad* :(A photo of Abigail in a tiny coffin with a tiny bouquet in her hands. Caption: *Don't these flowers bring out the beautiful violet of her bruises?* A photo of Abigail being lowered into a grave. Caption: *Poor Abby. It was an accident. She had been fed earlier. How strange that she escaped. No one's fault.*

I hadn't even had to use my knife after all.

The Moor

Elin Olausson

Elin Olausson is a horror writer. She lives in Sweden.

We live on the Moor. Grandma used to say that water flowed here in the olden days, stubborn river water with strong fists. She knew everything about fists, Grandma did. The river was a storm beast, a blind rage, but now it is nothing at all and Grandma has ended up in the same dense dark earth it once tore apart. We buried her on the southside of the Church Rock, because that was how she told Dorte that it should be done. Every Sunday Dorte, my sister Dorte, stands in front of the Rock and sings. She does it at dawn and when I explain to her that it disturbs my sleep, she replies that things can't be done differently. Tyra sleeps like a corpse and can show the whites of her eyes like a corpse, too. My sister Tyra has white eyes and Dorte sings God-songs before anyone else has risen.

Tyra takes care of the rabbits. The grindstone stands in our shed, made of sandstone from the old quarry where Granddad and Great-granddad and all the other men used to work. The tools belonged to Granddad, too, the longknives and the hammer and the wood axe. Tyra is out in the shed a lot, but never Dorte. Tyra likes things that are sharp and things that are downy. Dorte sews clothing from most of the pelts, but sometimes Tyra hides parts and keeps them with her in the shed. She strokes the fur when she thinks no one is looking. The rabbits push through the earth that was once river—they are their own river in endless tunnels under my feet. I think that the rabbits should stay in their tunnels but I only ever tell Dorte, never Tyra. Maybe it's one of those thoughts I forget to tell anyone at all.

There is a road across the Moor but the ground is hilly between it and us, ridges with hunching trees and thickets lit up by poisonous yellow berries hiding the road from sight. A stranger knocked on our door once, when Grandma was in charge. I'm glad it happened then and not now when it's just Dorte, Tyra, and I. My singing sister and my sister with corpse-like eyes.

Granddad started working at the sandstone quarry when he was eight years old. That's what the men do, they break in the middle, and that's why we are girls and wouldn't have it any other way. The boy-Granddad bled from his hands and turned ugly and crooked. Grandma married him out of pity and had many children, who spread themselves out over the Moor. They are called Erid and Halvar and Meta and Laren and they are our kin. They have children who are our kin. I don't think any of them are as skilled at trapping rabbits as my sister Tyra.

When the Moor was a river there was salmon and trout and maybe pike—I've read the species' names in Granddad's book about animals. *Salmo salar. Salmo trutta. Esox lucius.* Maybe they didn't exist at all. Dorte says that the world looked different then and that Grandma liked making up stories. Dorte's head is as grown-up as her body, and sometimes I get very tired of her.

I'm good at hammering nails and at hiding. Sometimes I run all the way up to the cairn, and before they've reached me I'm hidden among the stones and invisible.

"Mei," Dorte says. Her voice is pointy and heavy, and her head jerks like an animal's. She's a large brown bird, my sister is, and I have to press my hands over my mouth to keep from giggling.

"Stupid brat," Tyra shouts and kicks into the dirt with Granddad's boots. This is why I like the cairn—no one dares to go near the rocks except me. Granddad never talked about the cairn and never looked at it. It has to do with death, but I'm too small to die.

"We'll go home without you," Dorte says. "Mei, do you hear? We'll leave you alone now."

"You won't get any food until tomorrow," Tyra adds. "Just sit out here. I hope the spirits take you."

I hear the slap when Dorte's palm hits Tyra in the face.

"Come out now," Dorte begs. Tyra stands behind her, covering her cheek—I see them through cracks and cavities. "You can't be in there. You know that."

The river flows forth when I close my eyes. I'll sing to it once Dorte and Tyra have gone.

***

I return to our house once the ground inside the cairn has gone cold and the earth has started squeaking. Dorte pretends as though I haven't been away but Tyra glares. Meat juice runs from her mouth, shiny with grease. She's scrawny everywhere except for her swollen lips. After eating we pray, our mouths moving around the words at different speeds. It's forbidden to open your eyes during prayer, but they don't know that I do it so it doesn't matter. Once Tyra peeked, too—we looked at each other. Murmured the words like Dorte does and sat there with our eyes open.

"You'll help me with the dishes, Mei," Dorte says and looks straight at me. Prayer is over. I lower my hands into the dishpan and wonder if the water in our well is river water. Fairytale water. I stay there longer than I need to just to feel it between my fingers.

We sleep in the room that has always been ours. Sometimes Tyra sleeps out in the shed and sometimes Dorte doesn't sleep at all. I'm always where I'm supposed to be. My eyes are heavy but I hear that hum from the earth, and I listen to it. I sink, cold and blue and lonely.

***

It's morning. We eat greasy bread, and drink, and go to the hole behind the house. Dorte has a tiny brush to clean her nails with. Tyra sits with her legs spread and carves at a piece of wood, her face as rough and knotty as Granddad's. She aims longlegged kicks at me when I ask her to tell me a story. Summer mornings, fall mornings—the year takes giant leaps around the house, and sometimes I run to the cairn. Their voices follow, Dorte's tired and Tyra's angry. Tyra wants to throw sharp sticks at the cairn but Dorte stops her. The river murmurs through the night and I wonder if Tyra would let me have a woolly little rabbit to tame. No, I don't wonder. I know.

***

The road lies splayed out beyond the hills, ugly and uneven. Dorte goes to the road sometimes but Tyra and I never go with her anymore. We went with her once but we never do it now. There is a woman who sells fabrics, Dorte waits for her. Returns with thin strips of colored linen that's no good for anything but mending tears. The woman is old, as thin as her fabrics, but with a swollen lump of a stomach. She walks very slowly. Dorte comes back with her colors and the woman's chatter like fluttering bird wings in the air around her. When the words flutter in my ears

I search the river instead. We live on the Moor. We don't need anything but the Moor.

It's from the road he comes. The stranger. He comes on Fabric Day and Dorte stands by the road beyond our hills with her basket. I'm in the kitchen and Tyra in the shed when she returns, without fabrics but with the stranger in tow. He's a man with long legs and boots. There hasn't been any man here since Granddad. And Dorte claims to revere the Church Rock! She throws her braids around, and the basket hangs empty and forgotten over her arm. Tyra comes inside and puts her knife away on the window sill. Blood dribbles over the wood—she's been busy. No one is as skilled at trapping rabbits as she is.

"It's ruined now," Tyra says, watching Dorte and the stranger.

I want to run to the cairn and hide, but now Tyra is here and would catch me if I tried. She never scrubs her nails like Dorte does and they are black, thick and long. She's quick and mean most of the time.

Dorte enters together with the man. Her voice is light and syrupy, false. The man has to hunker down inside the house—he's taller than Granddad. Taller than Granddad's sons, the ones that spread out over the Moor.

"Matteus," Dorte says and he grins with a too-wide mouth and too-white teeth. "His name is Matteus. Will you make the tea, Mei?"

The stranger's head moves in all directions as he surveys the lamp and the rugs and the knife on the sill. "You hunt?"

"It's just Tyra," Dorte tells him. "This is my sister Tyra, and that's Mei."

"Not what I'd expected out here on the Moor." What does he know about the Moor, this stranger? "I've passed this place many times, but your cottage isn't visible from the road. There are people further down, towards the woods. I usually speak a word with them when I walk past, but up here I've never seen a living soul until today."

I slam the cups against each other in the cupboard. Dorte doesn't seem to notice.

"Granddad built away from people," she says as if we talk about Granddad with anyone. "It's a good house, it's been here for a long time. So has the shed."

The stranger looks a fool when he smiles. His lower lip isn't beautiful like Tyra's, just fat and spongy. "To think that you live out here alone, three girls. Not bad."

I drop the tea tin on purpose, crushing the leaves between my fingertips. The counter turns grey and grainy. "We've only got three cups," I say, and Dorte's eyes sharpen.

"We have five, so you just take four of those." She's impatient, not as sweet-voiced as when she's talking to the stranger.

We only have three cups. The two at the back of the cupboard belong to Grandma and Granddad, and we never use them. When Granddad passed, Grandma pushed his cup to the back of the cupboard, and when Grandma passed, Dorte did the same with hers. The Granddad cup is blackened on the outside from all the fires he's heated it over. The Grandma cup has a dent on one side. They are Granddad's and Grandma's, and that's why they can't be used by anyone else.

"Not the Grandma cup," I say.

"Grandma knew what hospitality meant." Dorte comes up to me and takes the cups out herself. Places them on the table. "That's more than you know."

I'm not trusted with a single thing after that. Dorte pours steaming tea into the cups and shows the stranger to the seat of honor. Tyra sits by the window, quiet. I'm by the door, though Dorte tries to push me around with her glares.

Dorte wants to know why the stranger walks across the Moor. He tastes his tea. His hands are too big for the Grandma cup—they cover it until it's gone.

"I'm from a village far away from town, so I go there once in a while to see my old mother. The bus fare is too costly for me, and even if you take the bus you have to walk the last mile or so. I've always been fond of the Moor. There's a sort of serenity here, I like that. No sounds, nothing. It allows you to think."

I have to speak. "There are plenty of sounds on the Moor. The earth squeaks, it whines, it lives. The soil buzzes because of the river but I bet you can't hear it, since you don't belong here."

Dorte flies from her seat. "Stop it with that river talk!" Her voice is loud, almost a scream. "It's a story, Mei, don't you understand? Don't you understand anything?"

Tyra laughs. She draws her knees to her chin and laughs, low and croaky like a bird.

"I do understand," I say and go outside. Once I've closed the door I run, past the shed and the Church Rock, toward the cairn. I fight my way inside and I'm hidden. Invisible.

The door to the house opens. Their voices trail toward me, mingling with the sound of stomping feet.

"...just a child," the stranger says. Some words reach me but not all. "Could get sick...the earth is cold."

"Damn kid!" Tyra calls, and Dorte looks like she wants to do the same. They come up to the cairn, all three of them, stopping in front of it. One tall, black shadow and two little ones.

"Sorry, but I don't see what the problem is." The stranger laughs. "The girl is right there. I can see her watching us."

Dorte turns her eyes away from the rocks. Murmurs, "She's not allowed...it's no place for us. She's not supposed to be there."

"Damn kid," Tyra says again, but this time her voice is almost sad.

The stranger's laughter hits us again. "What, you believe such old nonsense? It's just a heap of stones, nothing more. You can't be serious."

Dorte tightens her hands to fists. "It's the resting place of the fathers. It's the sacred place. The women can only touch the stones when a man of the family is to be buried—the men can't ever go up here. The spirits watch, they make sure things are done correctly. Grandma taught us that night when it was Granddad's turn to rest. We have tools in the shed—hoes and spades. We have what we need."

"Mei ruins everything," Tyra says. "Mei doesn't know how things are supposed to be."

The stranger steps forward. "You're lucky that I came by. I'm not afraid of any old superstition. Your spirits may do their best to fight me." He comes all the way up to the cairn. I don't have time to back away before he reaches into my hole and grabs my ankle. His other hand comes for me too and he pulls, stronger than me and the cairn together. I'm dragged into the open, aiming kicks at him but he laughs, pinching my arm.

"There she is. See, that wasn't so hard. The spirits must be asleep." He watches me with his wide face that is far above mine, halfway to the heavens. "You need to be nicer to your big sisters from now on. They know what's best for you."

Back in the kitchen, the tea has gone cold and bitter. I sit opposite Tyra because they've made me.

"You have to agree with me now that there are no spirits." The stranger eats—Dorte has brought out honey cakes. He's had three already.

Dorte shakes her head. "The spirits can't reach you since you don't belong to the family. You're not from the Moor."

"And little Mei?"

"Mei hasn't become a woman yet. No blood. Once you have your blood you're a woman, and then the spirits know what you are. Tyra and I can't touch the stones—they won't let us. Mei can." Her eyes harden. "But she shouldn't."

I have never heard the bit about blood before. I don't like it. "It's the river," I say. "It's because I can hear the river, and you can't."

The stranger laughs with his fat lips and pearly teeth. "Water out here? I'd like to see that. Dry as dust it is, drier than any place I've seen."

I watch him. Still, I don't see him.

He stays in the house that night. It's the kind of night when Dorte doesn't sleep. He doesn't sleep either. The bed thumps and screeches, and they make vile noises that slice through my head. He goes still after a while and Dorte rises. Her nightgown hangs off one shoulder, unbuttoned. I hear her walk out of the house and to the Church Rock. She's singing. The stranger sleeps but Dorte is singing. Tyra's in the shed, caressing silky furs with unwashed hands. She does it in her sleep.

It roars and rushes. I hear it over Dorte's song, over all the songs in the world. The river, the fairytale water—Grandma's promise. There has been a river once, and there shall be a river again. What once was will exist again.

It lies on the window sill, forgotten. The wood under it is dark and sticky. I grab it in my hand and it only weighs a little, is as light and soft as an animal.

My feet move over the floor toward the bed where he sleeps. I turn the knife this way and that in my hand. The earth laughs. The earth lives and breathes and waits for me to set things right.

Once you have your blood you're a woman.

Maybe it's the flowing blood I'm hearing?

Hubris' Nest

J.V. Gachs

J.V. Gachs a Spanish writer and latin teacher.

First appeared in Spanish in Los Cuentos de Niña Loba Editorial/1

Hubris' death caught us all off-guard. We couldn't take it in for a few days. That is, of course, the most logical reaction of an immortal tribe, such as ours, to the sudden and voluntary death of one of its members.

The morning of the tragic event had passed just like all the previous ones of which there was memory. We woke up when our eyes were hit by the light of dawn. We greeted with the due ceremony the Sun, the River, the Trees, and all the Animals with whom we share our settlement. We took fresh milk from the goats, cornbread and honey for breakfast. Then, as was our custom, we sat down, each in our designated position, to contemplate the beauty of the Whole and the infinity of Time. Hardly half the day had passed when Hubris jumped up.

"Well, isn't this boring," he exclaimed and fell dead at our feet.

Throughout our long existence we have witnessed the cycle of life of millions of beings, the rise and fall of entire civilizations, and the genocide of several warring races at the hands of other equally foolish ones, but never, ever, anything like that. It was something unusual that, by the mere force of his will, someone would cease to exist.

He had, moreover, the tremendous discourtesy of leaving his

body behind so that we would have to deal with him. We held an urgent meeting of the Council, but no one remembered ever having seen themselves in such circumstances before. Never had one of us left this world, for what we could remember at the time. We, therefore, lacked any form of funeral rites. On the other hand, we weren't very skilled in the art of inventing things out of thin air that did not serve some practical purpose, such as plowing or building shelters for the rainy season. All the options that were proposed during that meeting turned out to be fairly insane. No solution seemed to represent our beliefs. It was impossible to imagine with what new system of destruction of bodies we could feel comfortable if a similar incident ever happened again. All that remained for us was imitation.

First, we tried to burn it, which seemed to be the favorite method of most mortal tribes. After three days and three nights of senselessly wasting wood, it was clear that this was not going to work. The flames floated around Hubris with no other effect than providing a beautiful purple light during the nights of the cremation attempt. His body remained so young and smooth after we got tired of chopping wood and throwing it into the pile as the day he had died.

Our next resort was to bury him. Recently, we had attended a number of mortal funerals where this method had been adopted. It seemed to serve the purpose of keeping the perished close to the tribe in order to visit and honor them. With that intention we built for him a clay box where we deposited him along with his most precious possessions: the feather of the falcon that once landed on his shoulder, and a stone necklace. This must have belonged, without a doubt, to some mortal. A gift from the time when we still loved them, when we suffered for them, before learning that our time and theirs are as different as that of the elephant and the moth. The point is the burial didn't work out, either. Digging a hole in the Earth for Hubris to rest and cover it up again was a long, tedious and, above all, very tiring process. When, the next morning, we discovered with disgust that the Earth had expelled him from its bosom, we did not even consider the possibility of trying again. It wasn't worth wasting any more of our sweat.

We wanted to give him to the river that crosses our land, then. Our intention was that Hubris would be carried to the Sea where he would become part of the Whole when he was devoured by fish. We thought that, at last, we had found the perfect solution. One that completed the cycle of life. We placed him on a raft built especially for the occasion with the most beautiful trees we could find. Without sparing any effort, we looked for flowers of all kinds growing on both sides of the river and covered him with them carefully. But once we placed the raft on the water, instead of moving away towards the sea, Hubris' body looked like a salmon going up the rapids, refusing to abandon us.

Lacking better ideas, and, frankly, fed up with all that, we left him leaning against a tree, right there, by the river, hoping that, on the least expected day, his lifeless body would also get bored and decide to go away looking for adventures.

Several nights later, with his immortal remains still on the shore, we realized the main problem that Hubris' death represented for our tribe. Now we were an even number. At the first Council we held after his death, where we would decide which grain to plant that season, we were sadly surprised by a tie between the wheat and the corn. We repeated the vote day after day, each of the two factions sure that, had he been among the living, they would have had him on their side. The arguments ranged from the bread that Hubris liked to eat for breakfast to how much he liked the color of the fields of one or another cereal. No one could say that any of these statements were lies, but none seemed to be sufficient reason to tip the balance. We even, on one shameful occasion, raised our voices and used an almost belligerent tone, tired of so much voting.

One of us remembered then that, in the old times, so old that they were already getting lost in the mist of oblivion, there was in our tribe the custom of begetting new beings, in a similar way as mortals and animals do. By putting our collective memory to work we were able to remember in disgust how new lives were conceived. That nauseating practice had been, incredibly, one of our main distractions when we were still a young race on this world. Some of us went so far back in our memories that we realized, to everyone's surprise, that at the dawn of creation, we had been mortal like everyone else, until we were forbidden to enter the Underworld—a very sad story that I will tell you some other time. We concluded that it was because of such a ban that the body of the deceased remained among us, not because it resisted abandoning us by proving to be more stubborn dead than alive, but because it simply had nowhere else to go. Such revelations turned out not to be able to solve our problem. Even if that same day we had managed to conceive a new member for our tribe, something very difficult, this one would not have matured to vote before the harvest.

We remained silent until the words *anger* and *selfishness* were born in our language, with which we could finally express how we felt about Hubris' decision to suddenly drop dead. We headed to the river ready to do whatever it took to bring him back to life, and if he was bored, well, let him hold it in like everyone else. We even resolved to resort to magic if there was no other choice, something that had not been necessary since the last invasion attempt by a mindless human tribe. Fortunately, on this occasion, it was not necessary to resort to such drastic measures. A woodpecker had made its nest on Hubris' head, which remained leaning on the tree where we had left it. The bird looked at us with interest. We saw an opportunity and took advantage of it. We carefully placed a grain of corn and a grain of wheat in front of the animal in the hope that it would break the tie. That season, we planted wheat in the Valley.

Little by little, vegetation covered Hubris' body until nothing of what he had once been could be seen. That woodpecker left, but others came and then others. As we drew almost every time we had to make a decision, in the end we always ended up celebrating the Council around him. With the vote in favor of the bird in turn, we decided that once every cycle, on a full moon like tonight, we would gather here, around Hubris' Nest, and tell the story of how we came to leave the decisions of the Council in the hands of a bird so as not to allow this story to become a legend and disappear into the labyrinths of memory.

Heaven-Bound

Hayli McClain

Hayli McClain earned her BA in Creative Writing from Susquehanna University. She's been published in places like Flash Fiction Magazine, Whitewall Review, and The Molotov Cocktail. She and her friends dream of book deals, next.

Ann didn't know where she was going, but it didn't matter, so on she went on, deeper into the semi-dark of the woods. Shafts of moonlight guided her. She buried her hands in her pockets, hoping to disappear somewhere along the way.

Two hundred and thirty-eight thousand miles above her, the moon was not going anywhere. Fixed in place by the pull of the Earth, she heard—but did not heed—the many cacophonous rackets of human society. The bus-beeps. The over-phone arguments and the in-person arguments. Shouting, yelling, grumbling, seething. Dinging alarms to wake up, go to sleep, take dinner out of the oven, type that email (TAP-TAP-TAP), or change the channel from one jarring crash of noise to the next. Human-made music, blasted into ears, across rooms, through engine-revving, coughing cars.

The moon listened beyond all that...

Ann itched at the humidity in her hair. She'd left the ruckus of the indifferent city and its indifferent university behind her, at the foot of the mountains. Now, there was relative quiet. The birds had gone back to their nests. The first-chairs of the grasshoppers' orchestra began their solos, and the crickets applauded them.

Stopping between tree roots, Ann tilted back her head to gaze at the stars. Polaris, Sirius, Betelgeuse—her only lasting lifelong companions. Even though they never did much for her, really. Only make her ache. Only make her lonelier on cloudy nights.

If Ann ever *did* go missing, no one would notice. No one would look. After all, what was a girl disowned by her family? What was a girl too cautious now to make any connection with anyone? She'd left no friends in her hometown and she'd found no friends at college. She ate less. She slept less. She cared less. She couldn't carry on this way—financially, emotionally, socially, physically—so Ann willed herself to float away into the cold of the stars she'd worshipped all her life. To just fade off, quietly, into the purled stitches of the universe.

"Shit fuck!"

Ann jumped.

"Bastard of a thing!"

If any weevils were offended by the desecrated peace, they didn't say. Once Ann recovered from the jump-scare of it, she only felt curious. Silence, isolation, sorrow—those were a dime a dozen in Ann's life, anyway. It wasn't every day that someone snarled "bastard of a thing" from somewhere deeper in the woods.

Ann followed the sounds of struggling. In a small clearing up ahead, she found a woman yanking furiously on a rope, the other end of which disappeared high into the trees.

She was a stray cat of a woman. Every well-worn seam of her clothes spoke of belonging nowhere to no one, yet her eyes burned with vigor. She and Ann were the same age, probably, but those twenty-three years hadn't treated each the same. The woman's wiry arms were strong; whatever she was trying to pull down from the trees had to be stuck damned good for her heel-grinding efforts to prove fruitless.

"For fuck's sake." The woman let go of the rope, sighing sharply. She put her hands on her hips and stared upward between the boughs, panting, reevaluating.

"Are you okay?" Ann asked, from the edge of the moonlight.

The other woman startled like a stray, too, hackles up and poised for a fight. When her eyes pinpointed Ann in the shadows, she relaxed. Ann clearly didn't fall into the category of "threat," with her braided pigtails and hike-bruised shins.

The woman with the rope sighed again.

"Yeah, sure," she said. "But I could use a hand."

"With what, exactly?" But Ann was already hurrying over, dog-whistled by the wild-haired woman's take-no-shit, give-no-shit voice.

"You're a university kid, aren't you?" the woman asked, instead of explaining herself.

Ann nodded, blushing. Was it that obvious? Did she have the face of a dork, the smell of dorm on her clothes?

"Then don't bother asking." The woman rubbed her fingers together. "You'd have some smart-ass thing to say about it, I'm sure. Percy, by the way."

She held out a rope-raw hand. Ann accepted it, and maybe it was some fissure in reality or maybe she was going crazy, but it seemed as if the meeting of their skin added more music to the night. The last wakeful cicadas, the turning-over of dirt in mole dens, and *this*. Touch, spark, eyes meeting; someone stumbling miraculously into someone else's life.

"Percy," Ann repeated.

"Short for Persephone," Percy explained, "which is loathsome, obviously. And you? What's your misfortune?"

"Ann."

"Short for?"

"Short for They Must Have Been Low On Ink The Day I Was Born."

Percy's laugh cracked out against the night-song, loud and real and wander-weary. She shook her head, but it was the kind of *no* that meant *yes*. Yes, that was a good one.

"Ann," Percy said, another note in the symphony, "I'm trying to pull down the moon."

Somewhere by water, a skeptical bullfrog went *hrrmmm, hrmmmm* into the silence.

"I'm sorry, what?" Ann asked.

"I'm trying. To pull down. The moon."

Ann tried and failed to reconcile that sentence in her head. She could get by for the first two thirds of it. "The moon" sent it scattering out of her grip again, logic unspooled, no sense to be had. Pull down the moon? Was that supposed to be some kind of riddle? Not based on Percy's expression: one brow raised, grimly awaiting a smart-ass retort. Ann fought against every urge to deliver it.

"But that's impossible," she said eventually.

"Impossible!" Percy scowled. "It was impossible for man to talk until he opened his mouth. Now it's impossible to shut him up again."

"You did say 'pull down the moon,' right?"

"Yes."

"As in, the moon in the sky? Waxes and wanes? We landed on it, once?"

"That's the one, yes. Not any of those *other* shit moons you're thinking of." Percy's haughty, straight-faced humor was in total contrast to the absurdity of her proposition. It made Ann giggle. It made her give in.

"Okay," she said, "and why do you want to do a thing like that?"

To Ann's surprise, Percy answered by grabbing her arm and pulling her close. She bent down a fraction, so their heads bopped together at the same level. Percy smelled like pine, like soil. A woman of the earth. Her temple fit flush against Ann's.

Ann held her breath.

"Listen," Percy whispered. *"Listen...."*

She pointed to the ground beneath their feet.

Ann couldn't hear anything except the hoot of an owl some distance away, and then a fox yapping in heat or in hunger. The usual katydid musings. The moving of blood through her veins and the softer-than-soft ins and outs of Percy's breath.

"The earth sings," Percy whispered. "Not its critters. I mean, *they* sing, obviously. *We* sing. But the Earth herself—she sings, too, and no one listens except the moon, because she loves her."

Ann gazed upward.

She couldn't see the moon from that angle. But spread through the sky across from it, Ann could see the motley, mythos-soaked parade of constellations. She'd chosen Astronomy for a reason. The science of it. The incomprehensible complexities of the universe waiting patiently to be discovered, explained, understood. Most of all, she chose Astronomy for its history of yearning.

Everyone who ever lived looked at the same moon. The same stars.

Ancient heroes, little lost kids, misfits, kings, killers, lovers—every one of them gazed up at the red furnace fire of Antares. Did they know its name? Did they know it was the Heart of the Scorpion? Probably not. Many of them must have had their own story behind Orion and his triple-star belt. Still, they had all followed that same sky-locked hunter of the stars as he pinwheeled from one horizon to another.

Ann liked Orion, but she'd always preferred Cassiopeia. Beautiful, vain Cassiopeia, bound to her throne of stars, her world upside-down for half the year. A queen punished by the scorn of men and gods.

What would Cassiopeia do, Ann used to wonder as a girl, if she were free?

"Can you imagine," Percy began softly, "being trapped in the gravity of your true love, but never being able to *reach* them?"

Ann didn't have to imagine it. She'd orbited that agony many times in her life, paired up with Becky Marckle for macaroni art, swapping songs that cautiously bordered romance with Phoebe Fletcher in seventh grade, comforting but never confiding to Viv Ryner throughout high school.

But those weren't true loves, were they?

True love wasn't a mopey middle school playlist abandoned by eighth grade. It was a song you never grew tired of hearing. It was Andromeda, Lady of the Heavens, forever reaching after her hero in the night sky. It was Altair and Vega, two stars crossed in love, and the many magpies that came to bridge the rushing Milky Way river between them.

"Will you help me?" Percy asked.

Will I be a magpie for the moon? Ann asked herself, and put *that* way, there could only be one answer:

"Yes."

She took the limp end of the rope and wrapped it twice around her wrist. Percy unleashed a feral smile. Her eyes sparkled with the greenish-yellow match-flares of surrounding fireflies. She took the rope, too, wrapping it, bracing herself.

They heaved together.

The heels of Ann's Nikes ground hard into the earth, and she tasted sweat off her lip. Behind her, Percy growled with stubborn determination. Humidity festered in their shirts. Their arms burned and began to tremble.

The utter insanity of what she was doing threatened to break Ann in half down the center, but if she had to go mad, she wanted to go mad like Percy: feral fighter for love, believer in impossible distances impossibly closed. She'd pull down the whole Goddamn fucking moon, or she'd give herself an aneurism trying. Her mother called her unnatural, once. Well, then, who better to break all the rules?

"*Come on, you great fuckin' beauty!*" Percy screamed. "*Fight for it! Just a kiss on the forehead! How long have you waited for this?*"

And something gave.

The rope followed them a quarter inch, a half inch, a whole. Ann stumbled to catch herself. The full moon was obscured, leaving them in new moon darkness instead. The sky rumbled, bass and biblical, and one by one the crickets and katydids trailed off in their song. Silence swooped first through the insect world, then through the animal one, then even through the trees and the dirt.

Silence, like empty space.

Like someone holding their breath.

"*Just a little more!*" Percy shouted. "*COME ON, BITCH, DON'T BE SHY!*"

The sky screamed. Ann screamed, too, as blood slicked her grip on the rope.

Wind whipped up without warning, thrashing the trees, making them hiss like a raging storm at sea. Birds fell out of their nests, flapping and squawking in every direction. Next came a flash of light—blinding white fire—and cicadas screeching out in confusion.

Then, all at once, the sky stopped, and the rope went slack.

Percy hit the ground with a lung-emptying *hnunn,* and Ann fell on top of her, tears streaming down her face from the searing burst of light that still layered over her vision, even as the world returned to darkness.

"Oh, my God," she said when she blinked the light away. "Oh, my sweet Jesus God."

There was no sky left—not any that they could see. Instead, the trees crunched and groaned, the peaks of the surrounding mountains quivering under the weight of—of—

"The moon," Ann gasped.

Like a grand balloon on a string. Like a dream. Like a this-doesn't-happen-yet-it-has.

The moon.

The Goddamn motherfucking *moon*.

Percy scrambled up from under Ann. She held out her hands as if for fight or flight or full attention. Silence. No bug dared to sing. No rabbit dared to burrow. There had never been a quiet like this quiet. Ann could hear her own heartbeat. She thought she could even hear Percy's.

Percy dropped to her knees, crying.

"She's quiet," Percy whispered. "Listen. The tides are still. The plates are steady. There's nothing but this moment."

Moon kissing Earth.

Earth nose-to-nose with Moon.

The heroes and lovers of the sky looked on with amazement. And, Ann thought surely, with hope. Moon-dusted hope like hers. The realization that "impossible" was a thing love scoffed at.

A minute passed. Or maybe only a second.

Then the moon drew slowly away, rising heaven-bound back to its place in the dark. Life on Earth depended on their distance. That was the curse of their love, and they knew it, and so the lips of the atmosphere reluctantly unstuck from the moon's craters.

The earth began to sing again.

Man screamed over her, out-blaring music with violence and wreckage and rules, and all the world's critters made noise, too: the rustling of fur-soft slumbering bunnies below ground, the wheedling of brown beetles in bark, the dark's finest night-hunters lurking through the undergrowth. Still, the moon heard the humming of her true love. Still, she teased her curling tides in return.

Percy picked something up from the ground.

"Look," she said shakily. "It's a moon rock."

She brought it over to Ann, who was still gaping dumbstruck on the forest floor. She pulled Ann to her feet, supporting her when her knees almost gave out, and she shook the moon rock until Ann finally looked at it.

"Have it," Percy whispered. "I'm an earth girl, not a moon girl."

Percy pressed it into Ann's hand. She didn't stop pressing it into her hand. She was, really, holding Ann's hand with a bit of the moon suspended between them. There was nothing but this moment, caught in one another's gravity.

Ann stared moon-eyed into Percy's face.

"Got something smart-ass to say, college girl?" Percy asked quietly.

Ann blurted, "Don't go."

Dots had come together, shining points of connected constellations, notes slurred along musical scales. Ann discovered herself for the first time, glittering, bound by some of the same stars as Percy. The opposite of fading. The other end of disappearing. She saw now that her story was one arm in a forever-narrowing V aimed toward an impossible point. What? Where? It didn't matter.

Another wild smile unfurled across Percy's face.

"My moon girl," she said.

"Stars," Ann whispered.

"Close enough."

The distance between them closed with a bridge of magpies, and the moon and the earth and all the lovers of the heavens rang together in a celestial song only Percy and Ann could seem to hear.

The Garden of Extinction

Sam Grieve

Sam Grieve writes fiction and poetry from her home in Connecticut. Find her online at Samgrieveauthor.com

First published in The Lowestoft Chronicles, Winter 2016

Sometime—in the night before her departure—Kedu finds herself awake. The moon, pale as a curl of a melon rind, hangs in a sulfurous sky. Kedu slides her feet into her clogs, makes her laborious way to the door. She does not bother to turn on the light. There is enough of it outside as it is, casting its poisonous glare through the glass walls onto her furniture.

Her studio lies at the far end of the corridor. An interminable distance. Kedu puts her head down, concentrates instead on traversing each gray tile beneath her feet. One. Two. Three. Her walk is barely a shuffle; it infuriates her. She had always been a quick woman, a dasher, a scrambler, but the medication they prescribe has made her slow. Or perhaps it is not just the medication. She had begun to feel it recently, the weight of her years. She grinds her teeth, takes another few steps. Seven was it, or eight? It is as though her feet are shod with lead.

She shouldn't even be awake. *The fools must have miscalculated,* she thinks, and the idea arouses the old rebel in her, sends a thrill scampering down her spine.

At last she reaches the door. She rests, worn down by the agitation of her heart, its painful deceleration, then forces herself onto her tiptoes to peer into the lock. The retinal scanner whirs a weary welcome. *Be quiet*, she orders it. Wouldn't do to have anyone else here, not now. Certainly not that obese nurse, who speaks to her as though she is a child but manhandles her with subtle cruelty. Horrible creature. Let him slumber on.

The door slides open. Kedu hobbles in. Shadows mottle the floor, like the corpses of slain ghosts. The world is full of them. She navigates her way between their dark shapes to her desk, where a painting, her most recent work, lies. Kedu puts her glasses on. The sketch will never be finished, and perhaps because she must say good-bye to it, she finally recognizes its flaws, all the things that once eluded her. But this is not what summoned her in the night. She turns from the work and opens the right desk drawer, pushing her hand deep inside, over all her antique things, her paintbrushes and pencils and inkstones and curling, faded photographs, until her searching fingers encounter silk.

She tugs at it. The textbook is wrapped up inside, very snug; the whole package is not that easy to extract, and as she does so, the drawer creaks, an awful, strained bleat, which makes her heart thrash in her chest. And then the parcel is free and on her desk, like a rectangular swaddled baby.

Kedu unwinds the scarf. It once belonged to her mother, and although it has been in Kedu's possession for five, maybe six times as long, it has never relinquished the influence of its original owner. She drapes it around her neck, sliding the fabric between her knuckles. The silk is as soft as a mothwing and quite as fragile—a jagged hole mars a corner; the fabric is literally disintegrating. For several long seconds Kedu just sits there, allows herself the luxury of being once more her mother's daughter. But it is not her mother, or even her childhood, but the book that clamors for her, that has broken her sleep in the darkest part of the night. She straightens her shoulders, turns to face it.

Insects and Diseases of Rice Plants in Japan by Akira Kawada. Her dear old friend. Not Kawada, of course, he was a ghastly brute, but the book, the book itself. She opens it up at random, discovers a frangipani, still moon-white, pressed between pages 61 and 62. She turns some more leaves. Ah, here are cherry blossoms, some perfect, others fluttering to dust. And there a few pages on—purple violets with tiger-yellow eyes, collected in the mountains. She smiles. The beginning of her affair with Murakami. Making love on a mossy rock, him stopping halfway to rhapsodize over a nearby anemone. *"Darling, don't,"* she had cried. *"Please! Don't!"* But he had clambered off her regardless to take a photograph, his pants around his ankles. What a fool.

Some of the flowers still harness scent. She lifts the book, flares her nostrils, inhales. Outside she can just make out the glow-worm glimmer of the Sk***eyes™, their zigzagging patrol above the vastness of the Conurbation, then notices with surprise the sudden roar of the aerial interconnector between Tokyo and Wellington. Why does she hear it now? The white noise of the world is so engulfing she is ordinarily deaf to it.

"I hope it is quiet up there." The words manifest aloud and the raw, unfamiliar sound of her voice comes a shock. Her throat convulses, contracts into a fist.

Of course it won't be truly silent. There must be pollinators—insects, animals, or versions thereof—but who on Earth knows? There is no official information available. No research. No contact. And yet how many people, her people, have made the journey? Countless, including Murakami, who left soon after their brief liaison, dancing up the gangway of the container ship on his little feet. He was charged with a rare violet plumeria. When she said goodbye to him, he was carrying the seeds in a vial around his neck. She waved him off from the viewing deck, recalls the sun glinting on that little metal bottle. What else? Oh yes, she was wearing a yellow straw hat.

"Soon you will join me," he had said in that final embrace, but she had seen the pity in his eyes. Or at least she imagines she saw it. It was so long ago, and she remembers so little about him. She counts on her fingers. The smell of verbena on his fingers. The mole on his right shoulder, slightly furry to the touch. That perfect anemone, hanging like a luminous yellow sun in dankness of the forest foliage. His pale backside.

Will he be there? Somewhere overhead? Or is it down? The stars and their incumbent planets look alike from the ground. Invisible. Would he even remember her? Ah yes, she recalls now, he had called her his "loam-soled lover." He had fancied himself a poet. A sound, like the rush of dead leaves across tarmac, bursts out of her. All that is left of her laugh.

Murakami.

Oh dear.

Outside, toward the bay, an interplanetary ship begins its searing ascent into the sky. It barely appears to rise at first, and she finds herself mesmerized by the violence of its amputation from the Earth, its baptism in cloud. Tomorrow that will be her. That uprooting. The grip on her throat tightens further. She shakes her head. No point in getting maudlin. What the hell is there here for her anyway, except the lackluster ministrations of her nurse? She must think ahead, as she always has. To the Garden.

She tugs her stool out, eases herself down, and turns another page in the book. Here is a flower from early in her life. A rare, tiny orchid, a flattened dragon. This one she had discovered with her grandfather on one of their excursions. Long, black socks pulled over her knees. Jiji's butterfly net jutting out from his shoulder—a single, quivering antenna. Jelly-filled jars, for cuttings, chiming like bells within his backpack. It was he who had told her about the Dryad Project, about the Garden. How it hung amongst the stars, remote, undisclosed, on which every extinct plant thrives, a celestial ark, pulsating with bio-flora no longer even imagined on Earth.

"Is it real?" she had asked him. "Really real?" And he had said, "Yes, yes, my darling, it is real as you and me, a beautiful, blue, living dream among the gas and rocks and dunes and dust and lifeless light."

"And will I see it?"

"If you are chosen," he had told her. "And only the most deserving are." He had lifted a strand of hair out of her eyes, smoothed it behind her ear. "It is like in the old legends. The garden is guarded by angels. It is a paradise in the sky."

Jiji was summoned three days before Kedu turned eleven. Her family was overjoyed; they released one hundred white lanterns toward the darkening horizon. She sat on the hillside and watched them, those ethereal lights sailing to their demise over the sea. The hill pulsed with the fragrance of wild garlic (oh, why had she not thought to save a flower for her book?) and cricket song, and, in the euphoria, her birthday was quite forgotten. She did not care. Jiji was gone and her heart was so heavy she could barely breathe.

This was when she began to suspect she was made of different clay. When others felt joy, she felt despair. What they accepted, she challenged. Not verbally, of course, that would be unthinkable, and she was barely conscious of her dissent; instead it manifested itself as curiosity. She longed to see where he had gone.

And so on the day she reached her majority, she got up early, caught the Transport into the Hub, and signed herself up for the Honorable Flight List. And then she had waited.

She had never imagined anyone could wait so long.

Kedu swallows. She has never been a weeper. Water is to nourish, not waste. She turns another page. Dandelions. She touches a finger to their crisp, tiny petals. These are later memories, after Jacques, after he had come into her life and then left, following Jiji, Murakami. Ten years. Ten years in a sea of years when she had been almost happy. There had been a moment of hope, then, for the forests and the oceans. For the old multiplicity. She and Jacques had worked tirelessly. She had decoded species, saved what she could. So what had come between them? She wracks her brain, remembers him sullen, drinking, his long, white legs stretched out. Her. He had been unhappy with her: with her success, her looks, her disinterest in him.

"You don't care for me," he had whined, but what he meant was, *"You don't cherish me. You don't elevate me above yourself."*

She touches the dandelion again. Funny that. That she now understands. *I was not the best of wives.*

She had not been the best at anything except her research, and in that she had excelled. She had been like a conjuror. Quadrupled the growth rate on wheat. She had fed the ever-growing populace. Why, it was due to her breakthrough that the End-of-Life date had been legally extended—to three hundred seventeen years! Double the previous allotment. All those living souls, nourished with her grain, her A-anion™ varietal. They were like her children, she supposed. She gave them life. And yet, ironically, she had never actually been a mother. Hadn't wanted children. Hadn't wanted anything domestic, to be honest. It had all been about work. Work, work, work. No wonder Jacques had left her, gone ahead.

She opens the book again, at random, and a Banksia rose, the color of her yellow hat, falls into her lap. She stares at it. Where had she picked this? Her mind is playing tricks on her. And then it comes back in a rush: Micou, her little sister—they must have collected this together. But where was it? She cannot remember. The fist in her throat again. She will not think of Micou, of Mama, and their conscientious objection. How they had chosen the old way. She had begged them to relent. Gone down on her knees and implored them, but they had been so stubborn. Perhaps she might have forgiven her mother, but Micou had been so young, so brilliant. It had seemed almost selfish. The way she had let nature take its course. Abandoned her only sibling.

Kedu closes the book with a bang, shoves it aside.

She does not know how much time passes, but at last the toxic glow of the mined moon dips below the horizon. Kedu glances at her console, at the time. She should be getting back to her room. Soon they will be coming for her. She reaches out a hand, hesitates, then pulls the book in close again, presses it against her chest. All these years she has waited for her summons, but now that it has come, she finds she is weak. Oh, it has taken her a long time, a lifetime, an extended lifetime at that, but she alone understands what the summoning involves. It has taken her years to work it out. No. No. That is not true. She knew from the beginning. When Jiji departed. When she was left with silence. She understands that now. She just hid that knowledge away. Wrapped it up in the carpentry of her heart.

Jiji. He had taken his butterfly net. His butterfly net! She cannot help herself; her dead-foliage laugh bursts out of her again. But maybe they were the lucky ones? After all, she thinks, they lost nothing. They feared nothing. The words of the song come back to her.

And the fools went first,

shooting like fireworks into the sky.

Murakami with his pitying eyes. Jacques. All those botanists. Those scientists. They had been so triumphant. So proud. They had had no inkling. None of them would have done what they did to the Earth if they had not been brainwashed to believe in the Garden. They were like children building sandcastles, she thinks. Stamping on their creations with joy because they could simply construct another one. But it was all a bluff. She is sure of it. A paradise? Oh, for Heaven's sake! She starts to laugh again, gasping now for breath. They had inherited Paradise! *The Garden* was a fraudulent insurance policy, not worth the paper it was written on. And being sent there was not an honor. It meant you were expendable. And she has not been expendable, until now.

***

She wraps the book up and slides it back into her desk. Perhaps the fat nurse will find it. He will inevitably go through her things. Maybe he will learn something but she doubts it. He lacks a recalcitrant mind. No, he will report her contraband all right, her illegal flora, but by then it will be too late. She will be gone, for soon, very soon now, they will arrive in a cavalcade, and she will be escorted out to the middle vehicle. She has already decided she will not bring her cane. She will walk out, down the path, with her head high, past the empty beds where, two hundred years ago, her campanula still grew. She will not let them take her hand. She will maintain the fiction. She will not let them know that she knows. She will be handed her Originals.

Then they will drive out to the peninsular, where the Pod awaits, gleaming like a golden egg in the dawn light. She will be stripped down to her bare flesh. She will be purified. And as the Pod rips its way into the sky over the fiefdoms of engineered soy and maize and wheat, over her golden empire of A-anion™, she will carry those seeds inside her, buried deep in her dust, her water, into Jiji's deathless sky. And for as long as she can, she will tell her seeds about their new home, about the Garden. She will tell them where they came from and how to flourish. She will exhort them to be brave. And she, Kedu, will be brave too. She will surrender herself to the dream, and she will find strength in it, as she has always done.

THANK YOU TO OUR SUPPORTERS

Many thanks to our patrons and supporters, especially:

Anna O'Brien • Cathrin Hagey • Kathryn Parsons
Amber • Natalie Weizenbaum • Johanna Levene

Aidan Long • Anna Evans • Bonnie Warford
D.M. Domosea • Erik DeBill • Felicia O'Sullivan
Frederick Stark • J'nae Spano • Katie Conrad
Kennon Hulett • Martin Cohen • Mollie Morgeson
Salomao Becker • Sarah Jackson • Lisa Cox
Tory Hokc • Steven • carol shoemake

Ally Shaw • BethOfAus • Brit Hvide • Carly Racklin
Charlotte Nash-Stewart • Dirck de Lint • Emily Anderson
GriffinFire • J. Askew • Jen G • Academia Alegría
Jocelyn Actual • Karen Anderson • Kristina Saccone
Leslie Anderson Maria Haskins
Matthew Bennardo • Rochelle B • Sian Jones
Suzanne Thackston • Wanda • Kayla • willowcabins

Want to see your name here? Become a patron!
patreon.com/lunastation

About the Cover Artist

Natasa Ilincic graduated in Cultural Anthropology at the University of Venice, with a thesis on traditional Balkan tattooing. Following her studies, she moved to Scotland to pursue a career in art and illustration. Her work, centred on mythology and inspired by dark corners of history and folklore, has been shortlisted for the Folio Society Book Illustration Competition 2017 and World Illustration Awards 2018, and exhibited in various galleries including the London House of Illustration and Somerset House.

Natasa lives in Edinburgh, with her partner and a little jungle of plants, and is the creator of A Compendium of Witches.

http://natasailincic.com

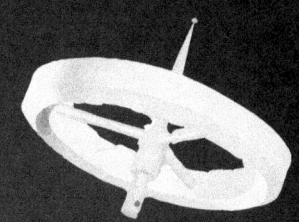

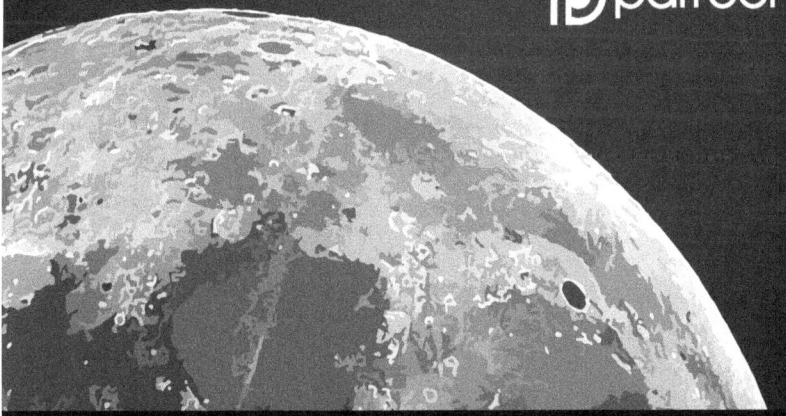